MW01004786

TELL ME THE TRUTH

KIERSTEN MODGLIN

KIERSTEN
MODGLIN
Love Lies Alibis

Cover Design by Kiersten Modglin
Copy Editing by Three Owls Editing
Proofreading by My Brother's Editor
Formatting by Kiersten Modglin

First Print and Electronic Edition: 2022
kierstenmodglinauthor.com

This one's for the inner voices we were all taught to quiet and the gut instincts we were taught to ignore. This one's for you. And for me. And for anyone out there finding their voice and learning to trust themself again.

CHAPTER ONE

I knew he was lying.

Though he'd perfected his skills down to an art —showing no signs of the falsehood on his face, not a hint of blush on his cheeks, or an ounce of fear in his eyes—I knew.

But he would cover it up as usual.

Fumble his way through it.

Find a way to make it all make sense. Or, sense enough.

And hope I'd be dumb enough to buy into his lies. I always had before.

Right on cue, he said, "I honestly have no idea how they got on my phone. Sam had to use it the other day when he forgot his. Remember, I told you about that?" I remained silent because he hadn't told me that, and we both knew it. "Anyway, maybe he put them on there as a joke."

"How would that be funny? Like, at all?"

"I don't know? To see how long it would take me to notice?" He shrugged, then inhaled. "It's stupid guy stuff, you know. But you're right, it wouldn't be funny. It *isn't* funny. It's stupid. I'll talk to him. It won't happen again."

"Joe, this just doesn't make sense. Why would Sam put pictures of some random woman on your phone anyway? Even as a joke? Who is she? That's not normal guy stuff... If he did, you should report him to HR. You're both teachers, for Christ's sake. Is this who we have teaching the world's children? A bunch of perverts?"

"Oh, come on, Edith, lighten up a bit. It's not the end of the world. It's a few photos. Nothing I haven't seen before." He gave an exasperated sigh, then narrowed his gaze at me. "Besides, why were you going through my phone anyway? Is that what we're doing now? Snooping on each other?"

Oh, so that's *what we're doing now?*

Hello, gaslighter.

I recoiled at the accusation. "I wasn't *snooping*. I wasn't even going through your phone. It vibrated while you were in the restroom, so I checked it. It was a text from Sara asking for a photo of your class for the school newsletter. I was going to send it to save you the trouble." I scowled, angry that he was forcing me to defend myself this way. "But, of course, when I opened your pictures...I found the photos. *Of her*."

He shook his head, looking away. "Okay, I'm sorry I accused you. I never look through my pictures, you know that."

"How would I know that?"

He rolled his eyes. "All I'm saying is that there are probably less than a hundred pictures on my phone in total. I don't touch them. I don't exactly do inventory on them. Who knows how long they've been there. Honestly, just delete them, okay? I have no idea why they're there or how they got there." He shoved the phone at me, his lips tight. "You know me. You know I would never do that." *Never do that again.* The statement was silent between us, but we both knew it was there. "I'm sorry you found them. I know it probably hurt and worried you. But you have nothing to worry about..." He trailed off, looking away, then mumbled, "I swear, I'm going to kill Sam." When he met my eyes again, he chuckled nervously, his hand raking through his hair. "I'll be sure to tell him you called him a pervert, too. He'll love that."

I wasn't laughing. Not even a smile on my lips.

He'd never admit the truth. I knew that. Just like he'd refused to admit it the many other times I'd suspected he was being unfaithful. The only time he'd ever come clean was when I found irrefutable proof. When I'd caught him red-handed. If he could find a way to lie his way out of a situation, he always, always would.

I laid his phone on the counter, refusing to look at the photos again. It would make me sick.

I couldn't stomach the thought of how many times he'd looked at them. And—at least most likely—seen the real version in person, too.

"I don't believe you, Joe," I said through gritted teeth. "You're lying to me. You're obviously having an affair. Have you cheated on me again? Are you sleeping with her?"

"What?" His scoff was loud and boisterous, his brown eyes widening. "Of course not. Look at me, *look*." His hands were on either side of my face then, and I tried not to think about where else they might've been. "*You* are the only woman I want or need. You know that."

I raised a brow, my chin quivering. "You are," he insisted, kissing my forehead. "I love you." He released my face and picked up the phone, swiping his thumb across it quickly. I couldn't see the screen, but I assumed he was deleting the photos. Confirming my suspicions, he turned the phone to face me moments later, a grin on his face. As if he'd made it all instantly better. *Poof.*

"See, all gone. And I'll talk to Sam."

I fought back tears as I spoke again. "Tell me the truth, Joe. Please. If you're cheating, if you're having an affair, please just tell me. I can't go through this again." *I'm not sure I'll survive it.*

He shook his head and kissed my cheek, his thumb

brushing over the place where his lips had been. "I'm not cheating on you, sweetheart. That's the truth. Cross my heart." He dragged a finger across his chest, proving the point as if we were in kindergarten, and slipped his phone into his pocket.

I could've argued, I really could've, and I wanted to so badly, but I knew my husband. It wouldn't do any good. Instead, I clenched my jaw and stepped away from him, in a hurry to leave the room. To catch my breath.

"Don't forget to text Sara that picture," I said, remembering the reason I'd had his phone in the first place.

"Right."

I walked away from him, understanding that he had no idea how much he'd hurt me. He didn't care to know. Never had. He'd offered me an explanation, and he thought, like all the times before, I'd just accept it, and we'd move on.

But this time was different. This time, I was going to find out the truth—not the truth he offered me, but the actual truth.

My dear, sweet husband had no idea I wasn't giving up so easily this time.

He thought he'd won. Cleaned up his mess as easily as pressing delete.

He had no idea what was coming.

CHAPTER TWO

The door to the break room opened, jerking me out of what felt like a trance. I knew something was wrong the second I resurfaced. And when my vision began to clear, I spied the dark-crimson stains on both my thumbs and a pointer finger. I'd been digging into the cuticle of one thumb with my opposite hand, pulling away the skin until I bled and not stopping there. Tiny, red blood splatters on the tabletop in front of me were just further proof of how long I'd been sitting there, oblivious to the pain. Nothing external could possibly hurt as badly as my insides did.

Jenna noticed the wound before I'd had a chance to figure out an elaborate excuse. "Oh! Edith! What happened?" She sprang into action, grabbing a handful of paper napkins and passing them to me. I dabbed my thumb, shaking my head.

"I'm fine, sorry. It's just a little paper cut." The

napkins burned the wound, and I applied more pressure, hoping she wouldn't ask to see it. If she did, there would be no way to hide the truth. She'd see the cuticle I'd torn open, strip of skin by strip of skin, without even realizing it was happening. It had been years since I'd picked the skin around my nails until I bled, years since my anxiety was this high, which meant I was having to relearn how to do this.

How to keep the old habits from surfacing.

How to appear calm when everything gnawing on my insides was anything *but* calm.

This was all Joe's fault. I knew that, but I couldn't say it. Not to Jenna. Not to Joe. Not to anyone.

At least, not yet.

She pulled the first aid kit down and laid it in front of me, then grabbed a bottle of bleach water and a paper towel and wiped the table clean, staring at me nervously as if I were a bomb waiting to explode.

Maybe I was.

"Sorry," I said again, landing on an excuse. "I opened my lunch, and it sliced my thumb." I pointed to the cardboard box for the microwaveable dinner in front of me.

"Ahh..." She tossed the paper towels she'd been cleaning with into the trash and grabbed a new handful, going over the table once again. The smell of bleach permeated the air. "Probably the least of the damage that meal's doing," she said pointedly, eyeing the cooling pile of macaroni and cheese in the corner of the tray. "You're going to start hurting my feelings if you don't quit bringing that pseudofood in here when you have perfectly good home-cooked meals available." She rested her hands on her hips, studying me. "Unless you don't like my food."

"You know that's not it. These are just easy," I said.

I meant, *These are what I can afford.*

"What could be easier than walking into the kitchen and asking someone to make you whatever you want? I've told you, if it's about the cost—"

"It's not." Now, I was mortified. Jenna had already been gracious enough to offer her employees to eat at the restaurant for only what it cost her in ingredients, but that was still more than the dollar I could get my frozen meals for. Five shifts a week and it would really start to add up. But I couldn't say that. She knew Joe was a teacher. She knew we weren't exactly wealthy, but she didn't know that I was a month behind on my car payment and only paying the minimums on my credit cards.

It wasn't that my boss wouldn't understand—she'd told me more than once that she would help out any of her employees if she could—but I couldn't stand that. If there was one thing I hated more than everything else, it was being pitied.

Well, okay, maybe being pitied came a little bit after being cheated on and lied to, but it was high up there.

"Honestly, I've stocked up on these, and I need to clear out the freezer space."

She was quiet for a moment, watching me, but eventually said, "Are you sure everything's okay?"

I nodded too quickly, and it didn't go unnoticed. She sat down in front of me, her eyes falling on the bloody napkin in my hand but rebounding quickly back up to study me. "You know you can talk to me, right? If something's going on or... If you need help, financially or at home—"

"No, it's nothing like that." I wadded up the paper towel and tossed it into the trash can before standing and making my way toward the sink to wash my hands. "Honestly, I'm fine. But-but thank you. It's really kind of you to—"

The door to the break room opened again, interrupting me, and a man I wasn't familiar with peered around. He wasn't dressed in the restaurant uniform, and his hand went up with an apology.

"Sorry, I was looking for..."

His eyes searched the room, lighting up like a child at Christmas when they landed on her. Joe used to look at me that way. I couldn't remember the last time he had. I didn't say anything, but then again, they weren't waiting for me to speak. I'd been all but forgotten as he moved toward her.

"Hey, honey," she said, standing to hug him. I turned away, continuing to scrub my hands, grateful for the interruption. They were quiet for a moment, and then I heard, "This is Edith, our newest employee. She replaced Nolan. Edith, this is my husband, Colt."

"Oh, right," he said when I glanced over my shoulder and flashed him a convincing smile. "Nice to meet you."

"Nice to meet you, too." I dried my hands faster, brushing them against my pant legs before extending one to him. He took it briefly with a small smile. He was kind, but it was obvious he had no interest in me. His gaze didn't linger. His touch didn't stay. He only had eyes for his wife—as it should've been.

Some women have all the luck.

"You ready to go?" he asked.

"I'll be right out," she said as he kissed her cheek.

I missed the days when Joe picked me up from work.

When he kissed me without a reason.

I missed who we used to be.

I moved past Jenna and toward the table, but when I turned around, she was still there, her eyes full of understanding. She wanted me to tell her the truth, but I couldn't.

I couldn't tell anyone.

It was too embarrassing. Too awful.

"You're sure you're okay?"

"Positive," I confirmed, tight lipped. "Go have fun."

"I can close up if I need to," she offered, though I didn't miss the hesitation in her eyes. "If you need to take care of something."

"What fun is being the boss if you have to do the closing shift?"

"Edith..."

"I'm teasing. I'm fine. Go. Have fun. I swear, I'm fine." I forced my brightest smile and, finally, it seemed to work. She retreated to her office long enough to scoop her jacket from the back of her chair and grab her purse, then she shut and locked the door behind her.

She hesitated a final time, long enough to say, "Have a good night, okay? Call me if you need anything."

"I will." I waved nonchalantly as she walked out the door and back through the restaurant. I'd worked at Jenna's for just two weeks, and I was honestly sad I wouldn't get to be there longer. She was a great boss, really. Though the hours were grueling and the customers could be demanding, it was one of my favorite places I'd ever worked.

But the place was a means to an end.

I needed to get to know the woman who'd been sleeping with my husband.

And once I found out where she worked, I knew I had to work at Jenna's, too.

CHAPTER THREE

W hen I got home from work, it was late, and Joe wasn't there. I didn't expect him to be, of course. As unconventional as it was, my husband only lived with me part time. This was his home, of course—his things were here, he paid half the bills, he fixed things when they were broken—but his parents needed him, too. And so, his time was divided equally between us.

When Joe and I first met, he was living at home with his parents. A few years before that, his dad had broken a hip during a bad fall, and his mother had been diagnosed with dementia, all within a few months of each other. Out of necessity, he'd made the difficult decision to move back in with them. So, after the wedding, it didn't feel right for me to take him away from them full time, and neither their house nor our apartment was big enough for the four of us to live together. It was the compromise we had to live with, and though I hated it sometimes, I knew it was the right thing to do. They wouldn't be around much longer, and they needed him right now.

Despite his flaws, my husband was a caring man.

I knew that.

It was why I stuck around.

Someday, that would be us—sixty years in our rearview mirror, a home that had our name on it, and children and grandchildren to take care of us. To remind me of why this had all been worth it.

Of course, there were days when it would've been easier to leave. *Most days, in fact,* if I was being brutally honest. But I'd always believed those who quit when things get tough were missing out on some of the hard-earned rewards that come with sticking it out.

I twisted the key into the apartment lock and stepped into the small, dark living room. It smelled of the chili we'd made for dinner the night before, but I disregarded that thought as I flipped on the light and immediately noticed the bouquet of sunflowers resting on the sofa table.

I moved forward, picking up the card and turning it over in my hands.

He'd scrawled a note for me:

E,
I'm the luckiest man alive to get to love you.
See you soon.

Love,
J

I placed the note next to the flowers, inhaling their scent and plucking away several dead petals. He knew my weaknesses—him being one of them—but it wouldn't work this time. I couldn't keep falling for his games.

If I did, I'd eventually have no one to blame but myself.

What's that old saying?

Fool me once...

I moved around the table and into the kitchen, opening the freezer and drawing out a frozen dinner. I popped it in the microwave and started it, then headed for the bedroom, where I undressed quickly and slipped into my pajamas. I tied my hair back into a messy bun and, in the bathroom, I cleaned off my makeup and slathered on some of my acne cream.

I'd thought by thirty, I'd be done with acne, but as it turned out, I was just one of the lucky ones blessed with acne and the beginnings of wrinkles all at once.

I pulled and prodded at my skin as I heard the microwave beeping, reminding me of the three-hundred-eighty-calorie dinner that was waiting for me. Honestly, sometimes I loved nights when Joe was gone.

Nights when I could pig out and look my worst and not worry about a thing. After three years together, I would've loved to be able to say I felt like I could be myself around my husband, but that couldn't be further from the truth.

If anything, I still felt pressured to look and act my best.

It's not like anyone could blame me for that after what he'd put me through. I'd thought we'd made it through the worst of it. Everyone says the first year is the hardest, but we sailed through the first year without a worry. It was the beginning of the second year that gave us the trouble.

We'd found our way through it, though, put it behind us, and—I thought—we were moving on.

But when I found those pictures, when I realized he was back to his old ways, things began to change. Something deep inside of me snapped. It was not the first time he'd cheated—I obviously knew that—but now I was beginning to feel sure it was not just the second, either. There were times when I'd suspected things, when he'd gone out late or when I'd caught a whiff of perfume on his clothing, but he'd always had an excuse, and I'd had the impossible task of proving something for which there was no proof.

Last time, I'd been dutiful. I'd accepted my responsibility in the situation—we didn't have sex enough, I didn't put in enough effort, I didn't try as hard as I once had.

But, when made aware of my shortcomings, I'd rectified all of that. I'd done everything he asked, everything he swore would make us better, though, in the end, it hadn't mattered. All of my efforts had made no conceivable difference in our marriage.

And now, here we were once again.

This time, I wouldn't be the doormat I'd been before.

This time, I was determined to find out the truth. And if it was as I suspected, if he was cheating again, I'd make sure to never find myself in this position again.

Back in the kitchen, I pulled my dinner from the microwave and tore off the top, taking a fork from the drawer and grabbing a seltzer from the fridge. I moved to the living room and sat on the couch, laid the cardboard dinner box next to me, and balanced my laptop on my legs.

I opened the browser and searched for her first name, which was all I'd learned: **Amma. Dale, Georgia.**

According to the internet, there were no Ammas in our small town, so it took me instead to a list of Annas that was entirely useless and paid sites promising to reveal private information about Amma from Dale, Georgia, for a monthly fee. I groaned, exiting out.

This was the problem I kept running into. Perhaps that wasn't her real name. Perhaps it was a middle name. Maybe she was a felon who had changed her name. I didn't know, and I was beginning to feel a bit like I was on a wild-goose chase.

It was by pure coincidence that I'd managed to find

her at all. I'd followed Joe on a night when he was supposed to be going to his parents' house and was surprised to find him making a pit stop at a restaurant downtown near the store I'd been working at for the past several years. I parked in the lot across the street and watched as he entered the restaurant and approached the counter. I thought maybe he was just grabbing dinner for his parents on his way out of town, but that was when I'd seen her walking toward the restaurant. Tall and thin, model pretty, with long blonde hair she'd tied back in a loose ponytail and a leopard-print headband tied around her head. I thought she must've been meeting him for a date—she was dressed too finely to have been headed in for a shift—but I sat long enough to watch her putting on the apron as she entered the building.

Maybe I should've gone in and confronted them right away. In hindsight, I kind of wish I would've, but at the time, I was frozen, full of anger and confusion. And still, I had no proof.

When she saw him inside, she walked straight toward him. I could see them faintly through the glare on the window. He talked to her for just a moment before carrying out a bag of food. Then, he'd headed out of town to his parents' house.

I told myself afterward that he hadn't done anything really. My inner voice was starting to sound scarily like him.

They weren't meeting for a date.

They didn't kiss.

They didn't leave together.

It was nothing.

The only thing I knew for sure was that he did, in fact, know the woman from the pictures. Still, if I'd confronted them, he would've lied. He would've told me I was being ridiculous. That he was just there to pick up food and she was an old friend. The parent of a student, maybe. So, instead, I watched. And then, four days later, I walked through those same doors for my first day at Jenna's.

When my phone rang, it startled me, and I quickly closed my laptop before I lifted my phone from the arm of the couch and checked the screen.

Dan's photo smiled back at me, and I couldn't help grinning. Even when I wasn't in the mood to talk to a single person on the planet, he was the one person I could never ignore. I swiped my finger across the screen, and his picture faded away, revealing a blurry image of him.

Instantly, I realized he was in the car.

"*Girl,* what are you up to?"

I folded my legs up on the couch. "Just got home from work. Where are you at?" I tried to spot landmarks out his window, but it was all a blur.

"You mean you can't tell?"

"Huh?"

"You don't notice anything different about me?" He placed a hand under his chin, batting his eyelashes.

"What are you talking about? I can hardly see you. You're blurry."

"Well, blame that on the shitty service in this backwater town." He scoffed. "I just had my hair done, and honey, it looks fabulous."

"Oh, fun." I took a bite of my food, running the spoon across my teeth. "Where'd you go?"

"I tried this new little salon on the square in Dakota. I'm dragging you with me next time."

"You mean you don't love my hair?" I teased, touching my bun. In truth, I did need to get my hair done. It had been more than a year since we'd been able to afford more than a thirty-five-dollar cut at the salon in our local grocery store. My roots were nearing my chin. Once they passed it, I'd likely get it cut short and then avoid the salon indefinitely.

"Honey, of course I love your hair. It's just that I love it because it's yours, and you're my best friend."

"Ha." I took another bite of my dinner, wrinkling my nose at him.

"What are you eating?" he asked, his eyes narrowing as he looked my way again and flipped on his blinker.

Tick, tick. Tick, tick.

"Pasta."

"Yum. I'm starving. Got extra?"

I lifted up the box so he could see it. "Sorry, it's a serving for one. But there's more in the freezer. Want to come over?"

19

"*Do* I?" His face wrinkled with mock contemplation. "Is Joe there?"

"Nope, he's at his parents' house for the weekend."

He nodded but didn't say anything. It wasn't a secret that there was no love lost between my husband and my best friend. But they were the two most important men in my life, and that wasn't going to change anytime soon. Like so much else in my life, I'd learned to ignore it.

"So, are you coming? Want me to pop a dinner in the microwave?"

"I'm like thirty minutes out, so maybe wait a bit. Hey, speaking of Joe, have you talked to him yet?"

"Yeah, I have." My response was curt, and he noticed right away. There was a reason I hadn't brought it up.

"And?"

I looked away, picking at a piece of fuzz on my pajama pants. "He says he was hacked. Or that his friend accidentally put the pictures there. Or maybe on purpose as a joke or something."

He gave a dry laugh that told me it was as ridiculous as it sounded. "Honey, please tell me you didn't believe him."

"Of course not."

"And you told him that?"

"I did."

"Why am I having to give you the third degree here? Tell me what happened!"

"Nothing really."

"*Girl...*"

"I'm...I'm still trying to decide what I want to do." I ran my finger along a scratch in my phone case.

"I see... And by that, you mean how you want to kill him, right? I vote for a sharp icicle. Have you heard about that? *Perfect murder weapon...*" He beamed at me. "And no one would ever suspect us. We're too pretty."

I shook my head, rolling my eyes. "Don't be ridiculous."

"The fact that that man is still breathing means you aren't ridiculous *enough*. If Nick ever..." He trailed off, running his tongue across his lips as his picture finally started to come in clear, telling me he was getting closer to town.

"I'll just talk to you when you get here, okay?"

"Okay... I'm twenty minutes out."

"I'll see you in ten, then?" I joked. Dan was constantly getting speeding tickets, and it was a running joke that he could make it anywhere in half the time.

"Only if I hit traffic."

I laughed, ending the call and placing my laptop on the coffee table as I dragged the blanket up over my legs, chilled both from the combination of the paper-thin walls and cold weather outside, as well as Dan's words.

My best friend knew me better than anyone, but I

could never tell him about the dark thoughts I'd been having when it came to Joe and his secrets. I was angry with him, sure. People got angry.

People didn't plan to kill their husbands.

I couldn't plan to kill my husband.

And yet, if there was one thing in the world I couldn't tell my best friend, it was the fact that those thoughts had crossed my mind once or twice.

CHAPTER FOUR

"Hi! I don't think we've officially met," I said, approaching Amma as she carried her latest set of trays back to the kitchen. She smiled, but it was stiff. She was busy, and I was bothering her.

Spoiler alert: I didn't care.

"I'm Edith," I continued.

"Amma," came her tight-lipped response. She placed the plates on the counter, tucking a stray strand of blonde hair back into her ponytail as she patted her apron, searching for her notepad. Retrieving it, she seemed to remember I was still there. "Sorry, can I help you with something?"

"Actually, yes." I thought quickly. "Could you tell me where we keep the extra bottles of ketchup?"

She sighed, glancing out at the crowded restaurant. "Follow me." We moved quickly through the kitchen, heading for the supply closet I'd already been shown twice. "We keep all the condiments in here. Salt, pepper, ketchup, barbecue sauce, and sweeteners,"—she opened the door, pointing to a shelf in the middle—"anything that goes on a table is right here. The rest is for the kitchen."

"Thank you." I grabbed a glass bottle, though none of my tables had requested one.

"Don't mention it."

She started to walk away as I shut the door, but I rushed to keep up with her. "So, how long have you worked here?"

"About four years," she said. "The restaurant used to be owned by someone else. Jenna and her husband bought it about three years ago. Me and Eric and Nicole,"—she pointed to the cook and one of the waitresses—"are the only ones who stayed through that transition. Theo came from a restaurant in Tennessee last year. Everyone else has come in this year."

"That's a lot of turnover."

"It's the restaurant business. Jenna's an amazing boss, but people can't survive on these tips forever." She pulled out a pair of one-dollar bills.

"Yeah..." My own pockets were lined with similar *tips*. "So why do you stay?"

Her gaze traveled to the dining room, watching her section. "Eh, it is what it is. I don't hate it here, and I have enough seniority to get the days I request off, usually. It works for my schedule."

"That's really—"

She inhaled sharply, cutting me off with a hand up. "Sorry, do you mind? Table nine is looking for his check. I'll be back." Without waiting, she hurried forward, already searching for the check in her notepad with a giant smile on her face. I couldn't help noticing the way she poked her chest out a bit more as she neared their table.

Judging by the diamond wrist cuffs and the fact that I already recognized this man as a regular in Amma's section, I'd say he was the type who left tips a girl could live on. Confirming my suspicions, I watched him pull a hundred-dollar bill out to pay for his twelve-dollar meal. He slid it across the table before standing and patting her on the shoulder. His hand lingered on her skin for a moment too long, and he leaned down, whispering something in her ear. She smiled and, as she did, her gaze flicked back to me.

Caught staring for far too long, I averted my eyes, following her lead as I moved to my own section to check on my guests.

"Can I get you folks anything else?"

"This brisket wasn't very good," the woman replied dryly, reapplying plum-colored lipstick to her wrinkled lips.

"Oh, it-it wasn't?" I stared at her empty plate, every morsel gone. "I wish I would've known. I could've had them remake it for you. Do you mind telling me what was wrong with it?"

She clipped the lid back on the tube of lipstick,

looking at her husband as if it was the most ridiculous request as she rubbed her lips together. "Well, let's see, it was dry. It was flavorless. It was cold by the time I got it—"

"I'm so sorry. I came to check on you after you'd had a few bites, and—"

"I'd had a few bites of my beans, not the brisket." She was already sliding the strap of her purse over her shoulder. She waved a hand over the plate. "We're not paying for any of this."

"W-was there something wrong with yours as well?" I asked the man across from her, who huffed but averted his eyes to meet the woman's. I went on. "I— Let me talk to my manager and see what we can do—"

"Talk all you want." She was up and out of her seat, nearly bumping into me as she stood. "We're leaving."

"Ma'am, sir, please, let me just get the owner—" They weren't listening, already on their way out the door, and I rushed into the kitchen, panic filling me at the possibility of getting fired over something so completely out of my control. "Where's Jenna?"

"Here I am," she said, popping her head around the corner in the storage room. "What's up?" She tucked a pen behind her ear.

I struggled to catch my breath, hoping I wasn't going to get in trouble as I tried to explain. "The couple at table twenty-two, she ordered the brisket, and he ordered a burger." She glanced out into the dining room, scanning the crowded space. "I'd already checked on her, and she said it was fine. But then she said it wasn't, and she already had her purse. I tried to get them to wait; I hadn't even given them their check. They—"

She put her hands on my shoulders gently. "Breathe, honey. Just breathe. I'm not understanding what you're saying. What happened?"

I drew in a long inhale on command, then closed my eyes and admitted, "They left without paying." Her expression grew grim, but it was obvious she was fighting against it. "I tried to stop them, but they wouldn't listen. I'm really, really sorry."

Her head tilted to the side as she processed what I'd said. "Why on earth are you sorry?"

"Well, I— I mean, I didn't stop them."

"Edith, I didn't hire you to be a bodyguard or a bouncer. It's not your job to physically restrain the guests if they're being difficult. If they decided they weren't going to pay and they wanted to leave without talking to me, there wasn't a thing you could've done about it, okay?"

"You're...you're not mad?" The commotion in the kitchen had slowed, everyone pretending they weren't listening in on our conversation. As the relief sank in, I'd begun to burn with embarrassment.

"Were you rude to them?"

"No, of course not!" I sputtered, shaking my head.

"Did you check on them?"

"Yes, of course."

"Did you refill their drinks?"

"I did."

"Then you did your job. I have no reason to be mad." She smiled, her kind, dark eyes drilling into mine in a way that made me feel safe. But I didn't understand. Even if she wasn't upset with me, she should've been mad. This place wasn't like the clothing chain store I'd worked for before. Every loss came out of Jenna's pocket.

"But...they stole from you. They both cleared their plates and left."

She shrugged one shoulder. "Maybe they needed the meal and couldn't afford it."

I stared at her strangely. "You're...okay with them stealing from you?"

She smiled, blowing a puff of air from her nose with a silent laugh. "No. Of course I'm not okay with it, but there's nothing that can be done about it now. Everyone has a hard time now and again. I'm very lucky to be here, doing what I love. With a great staff, an amazing family... There's always a choice in how we respond to others, even those who hurt us. I won't let others ruin my happiness, Edith. You shouldn't either. Now, if you see that same couple come in again, we'll try our best to make sure they like their food before they finish. But I don't want you to worry about this, okay? Just clear their table and seat your next guests." Her hand was on my arm again, and she gave it a gentle squeeze. "Don't worry about it."

"Okay... Um, thanks." I walked away, my heart rate finally beginning to slow down. I'd panicked for no reason, apparently, but I wasn't used to working in an environment like this. If someone stole anything from me, I'd... My throat grew dry.

Someone had stolen something from me.

Someone.

I glanced behind me, to where Amma stood talking with a couple at another of her tables.

As I reached my own table, I began picking up the napkins and placing them on top of their plates before stacking them gently. While working, I overheard one of Amma's guests asking for a new entrée without any onions.

They'd stopped her as she zipped past them, arms loaded up with plates, and she nodded. "Yes, of course. I'm sorry about that."

"I didn't see onions listed," the woman complained, trying to wrestle the menu from her daughter's sticky grasp. "He won't eat onions." She gestured toward her husband, who was in the middle of a call.

"No problem. I'll get them to remake it," Amma said, struggling under the weight of her plates.

"Please hurry. The kids' food is already getting cold, and we came to eat as a family, not separately," the woman told her, finally retrieving the menu from her toddler and placing it in the holder with the others at the opposite end of the table. The child began to wail, her cries echoing through the already noisy building.

"Of course. Be right back with it," Amma called out, turning to dash away.

I followed her into the kitchen, dropping the plates from my table into the sink just after she did.

"Eric, table nine needs a new steak, well done, and fried potatoes. No onions."

"On it," he said over the sizzling grill.

She moved to fill a few drinks, swiping the back of her arm across her forehead as she danced in place, obviously needing to use the restroom. "Here, let me get that for you."

"What?" Her brows drew down.

"You've got your hands full. I've just cleared my last table. I can take this drink to them. Which table does it go to?"

"Are-are you sure?" She seemed hesitant.

"Yeah, of course."

"Okay. Thanks. It's table five, two diets." She handed the two cups to me. "I need to get table five's appetizer put in anyway."

"I can do that, too, if you'd like."

"No, it'll just take me a second," she said, dashing away and toward the restroom. Once she was gone, I approached Eric.

"I need a steak, medium rare, and fried potatoes. Extra onions, please."

"You got it." He laughed. "People and their onions today."

I refilled the drinks and took them to the table, returning just in time for both meals to be ready. Checking over my shoulder to be sure the restroom door hadn't opened, I set one of the plates at an empty table and hurried to Amma's guests.

"Hey, folks, your server's really busy, and she asked me to go ahead and bring this over." I set the plate down. "Is there anything else I can get for you?"

The woman put a spoonful of macaroni in her daughter's mouth before peering at the food. Her mouth dropped open as if she'd been slapped. "There are supposed to be no onions in these potatoes..."

"Oh, really?" I asked, clicking my tongue. "Gosh, I'm really sorry. She put in the order; I just brought it over. No onions? That looks like *extra* onions, doesn't it?"

"And that steak looks practically alive. It's supposed to be well done. What kind of place is this where we can't get a simple meal prepared correctly?" She huffed.

"Do you want to just go somewhere else?" the man asked, finally off the phone. "Reggie's is across the street."

"Oh, I'd hate for you to have to leave. Amma must've put the order in wrong. I'm so sorry about that. Like I said, she's been really busy. If you'll give me just a few minutes, I'll get them to fix this. What was it that you were supposed to get?"

The man grumbled to himself but eventually nodded at his wife, who repeated the order once more. Moments later, I returned with their correct order.

"We won't be leaving a tip," the woman said flatly as her husband checked his food.

"Oh, no. I wouldn't expect you to. Again, I'm so sorry about that. I'm not sure exactly what happened, but Amma will be back with you shortly."

I scurried away, fighting back against the grin growing on my lips.

You ruined my marriage, Amma. I'll ruin your life.

CHAPTER FIVE

O n Sunday afternoon, I was surprised to find
that Joe's car was in the driveway when I got
home from work. When I walked into the house, I
heard the shower going.

What are you washing off, Joe?

Better yet, who *are you washing off?*

I placed my bag and keys on the couch and made
my way down the hall slowly, trailing a finger along the
wall. No matter how badly I wanted to hate him, no
matter how much I enjoyed his time away, there was
always a small part of me that was glad when he
returned. A small part of me that hated him being
gone. That hated knowing things had gone so wrong
for us.

I wanted my husband back.

Joe back.

The man I'd fallen so hard and fast for just three

years ago. The man I'd married just two years ago. The man who'd made me laugh like no other. Who'd consoled me just months after we met while I cried over losing my beloved grumpy old cat, Smoky. Who'd refused to let me walk across the threshold of our apartment after our wedding. Who'd brought me breakfast in bed for the first two weeks of our marriage.

I rapped my knuckles against the door, waiting for him to shout over the water.

"You home?"

"Yeah." I pushed the door open and stepped inside the tiny bathroom, staring at the faded shower curtain with his dark shadow behind it. "How are your parents?"

"They're good. Dad said to tell you hello." He slid the shower curtain to the side and puckered his lips, waiting for a kiss. I leaned forward, pressing my mouth to his briefly. Chills lined my arms as I did, a boulder of disgust forming in my belly.

"I didn't think you'd be home so soon."

"Yeah, well..." He shut the curtain again, returning to rinsing the suds from his hair. "I was planning to stay another night, but they didn't really need me. And I missed you."

I nodded slowly. It was no coincidence that he'd cut his visit with his parents short after our last big fight, but I didn't expect that to continue. It never did. Usually, after a fight, Joe was on his best behavior for a few days, maybe even weeks. When I'd caught him cheating, we made it nearly six months before he started to revert to his old ways. The sneaking around, the lying.

This time I hadn't been so lucky. Or perhaps I just wasn't as foolish.

"How was work on Friday?" I ignored the fact that he was still waiting for me to say I'd missed him too.

"Fine. I promised the kids if at least half of them passed the exam, we'd have a week of just watching movies and no homework." He shut off the shower and pulled the curtain aside, reaching for the towel that hung on the rack. "And suddenly, three-fourths of them passed."

"Imagine that."

"Right. So, it's been an easy week."

"Sounds like a good incentive."

"Apparently." He ran the towel across his face. "How was your weekend? Anything exciting happen?"

"Not particularly." I walked toward the sink and ran my hands under cool water, patting them over my neck. I should've told him I'd taken time away from the store where I'd worked the past ten years, trading it in for a waitressing job with half the pay, but I wasn't going to. Not yet. Our accounts were separate, so as long as I kept my half of things paid, he'd never know the difference. He wasn't the type of husband to show up at my place of work unexpectedly. He couldn't care less about visiting a women's clothing store anyway.

Of course, when it came time to file taxes, he'd

notice, but we still had months before that was an issue, and I didn't even know what our world would look like then.

He stepped off the bath mat, standing just behind me and meeting my eyes in the mirror. "I tried to call you last night." His arms slipped around my waist slowly. I held his eyes, not moving.

"I know, but I didn't see it until it was already late. Dan stayed over for the weekend."

His arms tensed involuntarily. "Oh? Have fun?"

"We did." I blinked once, waiting for him to say more but not expecting him to. He wasn't exactly in a good place to start a fight.

"I didn't know he was coming."

"Me either. It was a surprise. It was nice not to spend the weekend alone, though."

He rested his chin on my shoulder, huffing a sigh. "Are we okay?"

"Why wouldn't we be?"

He studied me, seeming to be deciding whether to bring up the obvious or enjoy the fact that we were no longer arguing. Somehow, not fighting was worse than fighting, but he didn't seem to notice.

He kissed my cheek, the warm, woodsy scent of his body wash enveloping me. "Just making sure."

"We're fine." I held his eyes again, silently begging him to see and admit the truth. We couldn't have been further from fine. We both knew it. His hands gripped me tighter, his arms snaking around my waist. He inhaled the scent of my hair, then froze.

"Mmm... Did they have food at work?"

"What?" My stomach flipped.

"You smell like fried food."

He hadn't said a word about the fact that I wasn't nearly as dressed up as I should've been for a day at the store. Probably hadn't even noticed. But I didn't think about the scent that seemed to permeate my clothing, hair, and skin lately.

"Oh, yeah," I said as he sniffed me again. "It was Desiree's birthday. Christina ordered in from the restaurant down the street. Really good food."

He was quick to nod, though I'd caught a hint of worry in his expression. The restaurant down the street was the same one I'd seen him visiting.

You'll have to be careful when visiting your mistress from now on, won't you, Joe?

"Smells delicious," he said, his voice low. Something darkened in his expression, and he moved closer to me, though that didn't seem possible. My pelvis pressed into the front of our sink, his warm breath in my hair. "And speaking of delicious..."

I jerked out of his grasp and away from him quickly, my body physically revolting against him. The rejection in his eyes was painful, even if warranted. I tried to cover it by saying, "I should take a shower, too. I feel gross."

That part, at least, wasn't a lie.

"Oh." That seemed to settle him. "Well, you should've told me. I would've stayed in and joined you." He ran his thumb across the top of the towel wrapped around his waist.

I held up a hand to stop him. "It's fine. It'll just take a minute. Then we'll get supper started."

He was still for a moment, watching me, and for half a second, I worried he'd insist on joining me in the shower. Instead, he ran a hand through his hair, water droplets dripping onto the linoleum floor. "Okay then." He moved toward the door, disappearing from sight before he called, "I'm not sure how much hot water's left."

He shut the door behind him, and I crossed the small space, locking it quickly and silently and releasing a sharp breath. I could hardly breathe around him anymore. Could hardly stand to meet his eyes.

But I had to do better. I had to.

I'd never make it through this if I didn't. And I had to make it through.

I turned on the water just in time to drown out the sound of my sobs as they began to tear through me. My body began to tremble as I stripped out of my clothes. It was as if I were pulling off my mask, stripping down so I could finally experience all I was feeling. I allowed myself that freedom so infrequently—only when I was alone and only for minutes at a time. Otherwise, I worried it would consume me, and I'd never get back up.

As the tears fell, I was overwhelmed by the realization of just how tired I was.

I was so tired of crying over him.

So tired of feeling like I wasn't enough.

I stepped into the shower, standing under the lukewarm water as, finally, I fully gave in to the sobs. I'd give myself five minutes to cry, five minutes to wash, and then I had to go out there and perform like my life depended on it.

CHAPTER SIX

"What would you think about me getting blonde highlights in my hair?" I asked, twisting a piece of hair between my fingers. We were sitting on the couch, picking at the last of our frozen pizza, when I brought it up. The randomness of the subject was apparent in his expression.

"What?" he asked, his brow wrinkling. Actually, I couldn't tell if he genuinely hadn't heard me or if he was confused by the request.

"Highlights," I repeated. "I've been thinking I could use a freshen up. Something blonde and light before spring gets here. I don't know. It could be fun, don't you think?"

He didn't look convinced. "Where is this coming from?"

"Oh, I don't know. Dan went to this new salon in

Dakota and seemed impressed by them. You know how picky he is... Anyway, he said he'd take me with him next time if I wanted to go. It's been a while since I've had any sort of freshening up. Maybe it's time." I tucked my feet in the cushion of the couch to warm them.

He twisted his mouth in thought. "What's wrong with the girl who does your hair now?"

"I don't have a girl who does my hair. I get whoever has an opening when I go in, and it's always someone new. And there's nothing wrong with any of them, but I'd like to do something more fancy, you know? I just want to make sure whoever does it doesn't, like...turn my hair green or something."

"Why are you wanting to change your hair anyway? You've always kept it dark."

"Not always. I've had highlights before. Before you knew me. I don't know. I just thought it would be a fun change. I could start saving now, and in a few months, maybe we could afford it."

He shook his head, sucking his teeth before he flicked my hair. "I don't know. Maybe. I'm not sure how I feel about you as a blonde, but I guess it's your call."

"You like blondes, don't you?" I asked, my tone light and innocent, but I saw something shift in him. He was stony for a second, then shrugged, looking away.

"I like *you*. I'll love whatever you decide to do." He reached over, squeezing my knee gently. Then his eyes widened. "Oh, I almost forgot."

"Forgot what?"

His thin lips turned into a smile. "I got you something."

"You already got me flowers." There was no doubt he was trying to drown me in gifts in hopes that I'd forget what happened. He didn't yet understand how different this was going to go than last time.

"I know. But I saw this at one of the shops downtown when I took Mom to her appointment. It was perfect." He was already up off the couch and making his way down the hall before I could protest or ask any further questions. Moments later, he returned with a white gift bag. He handed it over, and I pulled aside the seafoam-green tissue paper.

"You didn't have to get me anything..." I trailed off as I reached the gift, wrapping my hands around the glass globe and pulling it out gently. The snow globe was larger than my palm, with two snowmen on the inside, smiling in the center of a forest of bare trees. The bottom was pure white, aside from a few hand-painted pine trees. I turned it over, watching the snow falling around them. "It's beautiful," I told him, running a finger across one of the trees on the base.

"It plays music, too." He reached forward, turning it over in his hands and twisting the golden mechanism on the bottom. It played a familiar Christmas song when he released it.

"Thank you." I held it close to my heart. "I love it."

"It's been a while since we added one to your collection," he said as I stood, moving across the room to the small mantel on the far wall. I had thirty-six other snow globes in total from various trips and holidays throughout my life. My grandmother had gotten me my first one when I was eight years old, and for whatever reason, the tradition had continued.

I eased a Christmas village globe away from one with a family of penguins and placed the new one in the center, running a finger across the dusty tops. When I turned back around, Joe was watching me.

"We're going to have to get you a new shelf for them soon."

"I'm running out of room," I agreed.

"So, you like it?"

"I love it. Thank you." Even to myself, I sounded bored. I did like the gift, but my heart just wasn't in it, and I knew we could both feel that. Was this what it would always feel like?

Until you do something about it.

"So, what did you and Dan do while he was over?" he asked, changing the subject as he sat back down.

"Um, we watched TV, ate junk food, and he showed me some of his new videos for his YouTube channel. Why?"

"Just asking..."

I turned the question to him. "What did you and your parents do?"

"Same as always."

"What does that mean?"

Now it was his turn to sound bored. He scratched his eyebrow aimlessly. "I took Mom to her appointment and helped Dad fix a leak under the bathroom sink. They told me about their neighbor's yapping dog. Then I *met* their neighbor's yapping dog." He chuckled. "Just another exciting weekend."

Just then, his phone buzzed in his pocket, and he pulled it out. His expression was stony as he read the message, and I could tell he was trying hard not to react to whatever it said. I didn't dare ask as badly as I wanted to.

Not that he'd tell me the truth anyway.

I moved past him and sat down on the couch again. When I looked up at him, he was responding to whatever message he'd just received.

Was it her?

Probably.

If not her, someone else.

After a moment, he looked up, apparently realizing I was watching him, and cleared his throat. He shoved his phone back into his pocket without further explanation.

"Need a refill?" He pointed toward the plastic cup I'd been drinking my wine out of and picked it up without waiting for an answer.

"Thanks." I stared at the space where he'd just been, lost in thought. How could he be so blatant about it? Why wasn't he even trying to hide it? Was this how little he cared?

You teach people how to treat you...

I heard the advice in my head, advice I knew to be true. I'd taught him that this was okay. I'd allowed it to continue.

How much longer?

How much longer would I allow it to go on?

How much longer would I have to?

Moments later, when he'd returned, he handed my cup to me and pulled out his phone again. When he sat, he was farther away from me than he'd been before.

I noticed right away.

It was her.

That was all the proof I needed.

"Everything okay?"

"Hm?" he asked, not looking up.

"Who are you texting?"

He appeared confused but put his phone down on the arm of the couch. "Erika, from work. She asked me to cover the lunchroom tomorrow. Her son has an appointment."

"Oh, okay."

"So, what are we watching?" He pointed to the TV as the credits began to roll for the show we'd been watching. "There's a new *Shark Tank* I've been wanting to see."

I nodded, passing him the remote. "Your choice."

He turned on the episode without another word, but try as I might, I couldn't bring myself to focus on it. I was too preoccupied with a million theories about whom he was actually talking to and what they were discussing.

Several minutes into the show, he paused the episode and stood. "I need to pee," he said. "Be right back."

He set his beer down on the table next to him and stepped over my legs, which I'd propped up on the coffee table. When he was gone, my gaze fell to his phone, still resting there on the arm of the couch.

Was this a trick?

It felt like a test of some kind.

Still, I couldn't resist the temptation. I leaned across the couch, grabbing his phone and pulling it to me as I heard the bathroom door shut down the hall. I typed in the four-digit passcode he'd always used and stared at the screen.

I didn't have much time, but there was so much I wanted to check.

First things first, I pulled up his messages.

The name at the top was...

I gasped.

Erika.

I clicked on the message. Maybe it was a fake name.

She'd texted first, saying, **Hey, remember when I bailed you out of detention duty last month?**

Ha, how could I forget?

I need to call in the favor

What's up?

It had taken her a few minutes to respond then. **Ethan has a dentist appointment I can't keep rescheduling. We need to see the surgeon and he's only at the office a few times a month. Doug was supposed to take him, but he's coming down with something and I don't want to risk it. Any chance you'd cover my lunch duty tomorrow so I can skip out between fourth and fifth period?**

Ah, what's a kid need teeth for, anyway? He'd joked.

Funnily enough, they're pretty important. I can ask Sam if you've got something going on that hour.

No, it's fine. I'm happy to do it. Just remind me tomorrow.

You're the best!

That's what I hear.

That was it. The end of the conversation. And it

felt innocent enough. He hadn't lied. He was always the charmer, my husband, but Erika had five kids and a husband she seemed to adore. I couldn't believe I had anything to worry about there.

I closed out of his messages when I heard the toilet flush and the sound of the sink running. Before I locked his phone, feeling relieved, I swiped my thumb over, checking for anything glaringly suspicious, and froze.

On one screen, far to the left and completely alone, sat an app I'd seen only a few times before.

Dater

The bathroom door opened, and he was coming toward me, moving too fast for me to think. What was I going to say? What was I going to—

"What are you doing?" he asked, standing in the doorway to the hall. "Are you going through my phone?"

"Why do you have a dating app on your phone, Joe?"

"What?" He scowled. "I don't."

I forced the phone into his face. "You do."

He blanched. "No, wait... This isn't mine. I used to... I mean, I've used this before, before we were even together, but... Edith..." He looked at me, shaking his head. "I don't understand. Where did you find this?"

"What do you mean where did I find it? It was right there!" I gestured toward the phone.

He stared at the screen with quiet contemplation,

then his head shot up. "Oh! I'll bet I know what happened. I had an update done the other day. Sometimes that brings old apps from where they were backed up. No big deal. We'll just delete it."

"Do you honestly expect me to believe that? After I found the pictures and—"

"I've already told you the pictures were a prank from Sam. Hell, maybe this is a prank, too. You know how he is!"

I pinched the bridge of my nose, trying to think. "Joe, why would your forty-year-old, married, father-of-two best friend want to upload nearly naked photos of a random woman onto your phone? Why would he want to download a dating app? What part of any of that makes any sense?"

He was exasperated then, growing angry. "I don't know! If I understood the way his mind works, I'd be worried for myself. It's fine, babe." He tapped the app, and it prompted him to enter a username and password. "See, I'm not even logged in. It's an old app." He reached for my hand. "You're all I need, like I told you."

I pulled away from him. "I've never seen it before. Why now?"

"Exactly. Because it hasn't been there. And..." He drew the word out, running a thumb over the screen. "Now it's not there anymore." Turning it around, he showed me a blank screen where the app had been.

"See? Gone." His Band-Aid smile was back. *See, I fixed it,* it screamed.

But it wasn't fixed. Not at all.

He sank down on the couch, pressing play on the show. "Come on," he said, patting the seat next to him. "You're missing it."

No, I thought. *I'm finally, finally seeing it.*

CHAPTER SEVEN

I still smelled of fried food as I adjusted the heat in the car the next day, rubbing my hands together rapidly. Dark speckles spread across the white sheet of ice that covered the windshield, giving way slowly until I could begin to make out the sight of the restaurant from where I was.

I flicked on the wipers and breathed a puff of warm air into my palms, tucking them under my legs as I watched the door. When the windshield was nearly completely clear, I turned the heat down, adjusting in my seat and fanning myself with the collar of my shirt.

She should've been out already...

Just as the thought crossed my mind, the back door opened, and Amma appeared, her phone pressed to her ear as she adjusted the strap on her mustard-yellow handbag. Her bright smile made my stomach churn. What did she have to be so happy about anyway?

Steam billowed out the back of the luxury SUV she was headed for, the windshield completely clean thanks to what must've been a remote-start option.

She pulled a key fob from her purse, still lost in conversation with whoever was on the phone as she slid into her vehicle. She lowered the phone, and I assumed Bluetooth must've connected as she talked animatedly, flipping the visor down to check her reflection. She applied fresh lipstick and swiped her fingers under her eyes, nodding. As she buckled up, she fussed with her hair.

Where are you going, Amma?

Who will you see?

Why are you so worried about how you look?

As if you could look anything less than perfect.

Once she was satisfied with her appearance, she peeled out of the parking lot, laughing at the person on the other end of the line without glancing my way for a second. It was what I was counting on. Outside of work, I was invisible to Amma.

I dressed in dark, simple clothing while she chose bright, complicated patterns and fashions that had not yet made it to our small town.

I'd never seen her in anything but a full face of makeup, while I chose to stick to a pass of mascara and concealer so as not to upset my skin too badly.

She was beautiful and outgoing, able to make friends anywhere and with anyone, while I was anything but. I think that was what hurt most of all—

that he'd chosen someone so different from who I was.

What did that say about what he wanted in a wife?

Was it all just a fantasy to him? Or was he trying to replace me completely?

As she turned out of the parking lot, I put the car in drive, keeping a safe enough distance that I hoped she wouldn't notice as I followed her through the many turns on her way out of town.

On the interstate, I nearly lost sight of her as she weaved in and out of traffic, blaring her horn in direct contradiction to her bumper sticker that read Promote Peace.

I was three cars behind her when she took an exit thirty minutes away from the restaurant. I flipped on my blinker and checked my rearview mirror before sliding between two cars.

Off the exit, she turned into a gas station, and my heart sank. What if she wasn't going home, after all? Had I wasted all this time?

Thinking quickly, I pulled into the other side of the station. If I waited, there was a chance I might be seen. But this was a gas station. There were a number of reasons I could've been there. It might've been the biggest coincidence in the world.

I looked up at the glass window just as I saw a flash of her blonde hair whip past. She carried a bag of something to the counter, smiling broadly at the man behind it. Even from where I sat, I could see that he was mesmerized by her. He leaned forward on the counter, scratching his thin, scraggly beard before pushing his wire-framed glasses farther up on his nose.

She passed her card to him as he rang up her snack —*What sort of things do you snack on, Amma? Children's souls, maybe? Puppy tongues? Broken hearts? Joy?*—then waved with just her fingers as she picked up the bag and turned to walk away. His eyes lingered on her as she crossed the building and out of my sight. I backed up from my spot, praying silently that her next stop would be her house. I didn't have time to follow her around town while she ran various errands. Then again, maybe one of her errands would be with my husband.

What then?

What if this all ended tonight?

Was I ready?

I didn't feel ready, but would I ever?

When I finally spotted the bright-blue SUV turning out of the parking lot, Amma had dark sunglasses on, bobbing her head to whatever music she must've been listening to.

Are you a pop kind of girl, Amma?

Or do you prefer country music?

Maybe, like my husband, you never gave up the '80s hits you grew up on.

Maybe that's how the two of you connected in the first place.

I followed her as she got back onto the interstate,

wondering if she'd filled up on gas too or if the snacks were the only reason for her stop. If so, maybe the ride was going to be much longer than I could account for.

Joe would be expecting me home in two hours. I hadn't told him what time I got off work, but at the old store, it was rare that I worked past six. If he hadn't heard from me, it was likely he'd begin calling my phone by six thirty.

I drove in silence, hating myself for what I was doing.

I wasn't this woman.

Then again, no one is ever *this woman* until she's forced to be. No one grows up with dreams that someday they'll be following their husband's mistress around town or snooping through their spouse's phone. No one imagines they could be the kind of woman who'd feel unworthy and unloved and still come back, begging the person they love to take another chance on them—as if they're the ones who've done something wrong.

In truth, as embarrassing as it was to admit and as much as I hated myself for it now, I'd always believed women who stayed after they were cheated on were weak. I never understood or sympathized with stories of women who were cheated on over and over again and chose to stay.

How could you not see it? I used to wonder. *How could you not realize he wasn't going to change?*

But when you're living it, sometimes you can't see

the forest for the trees. And, when your heart's involved, you tend to make up your own forest and fill it with whatever version of the truth you'd like.

When you're calling the shots, living your life in the forest you inhabit, despite the glaringly obvious issues the rest of the world can see plain as day, well, I was learning that only you can say when your forest is worth saving or when it's time to light the match and let it burn.

These days, I regretted the way I'd talked to my former best friend when her boyfriend in college had cheated on her, the way I'd harped about her needing to leave. It was never that simple, though I would've staunchly argued it was until it happened to me.

I considered myself a strong woman.

I could change a flat tire and pay for my own meals —even if they were frozen—and I'd always lived alone before I met Joe. I wasn't an easy target or someone with low self-esteem. I didn't think I was the greatest thing to ever walk the earth, but I knew my worth.

Still, the cheating had blindsided me.

When I found the texts, hours, and hours of conversations between the two of them, I'd asked him about them, and he'd come clean immediately. He told me it was an ex from back home, someone he had run into accidentally, and they'd begun talking again. She was the one who got away, and he'd gotten caught up in the fantasy.

The woman still lived in Cleveland, where he was

from and was in town for just two weeks when they ran into each other. They'd exchanged several hours' worth of texts, and he'd flown up to see her once.

But that was it.

They'd slept together one time, and he immediately knew it was a mistake. He'd been dying to come clean, but he was scared to lose me. He was glad I found the texts. It relieved him of the guilt he felt. Finally, he could tell me the truth.

Or, so that's how the story goes.

He'd apologized profusely, taking every chance to let me know what a mistake it was, and eventually, we'd found our way back to a good place. At least, I thought we had. That wasn't long ago, and already we'd made it back here. Only this time, it was worse. This time, the woman lived here, in our town.

The last woman was a fantasy. They had a past, and he'd built her up in his head. But we were hours away, and nothing would ever happen again.

If he wanted Amma and she wanted him back, he could leave me for her. He could choose her. And there'd be nothing I could say or do to stop him.

Ten minutes later, I followed her into a busy subdivision. Cars lined the streets, making it so we had to weave side to side not to swipe someone. She slowed in front of a large, gray home with white shutters and a three-car garage. With nowhere to stop without seeming suspicious, I drove past, picking up speed as I circled the block.

When I made it back, I stopped the car four houses down between a minivan and a lifted truck with a sticker that read, **Adults on board, we want to live too**. Hidden in plain sight, I watched through the open garage door as she stepped out of the SUV, tossing her sunglasses back into the seat and slamming the car door. She carried a bag of generic peach rings in her hands as she closed the garage door and walked toward the house without bothering to check her street for rogue cars filled with scorned women.

When she reached her front door, it swung open, and my breath caught in my chest. The man waiting for her was tall with a thick head of blond hair and a lean, well-toned body I could appreciate even from where I sat. He was a perfect match for Amma if I'd ever seen one.

More concerning, he held a young girl in his arms.

Upon seeing her, the girl flung herself at a startled Amma, who caught her and kissed her cheek, running a hand over her hair. Grinning broadly at the interaction, the man stepped back, allowing Amma inside. He glanced out at the street, and I worried he'd seen me sitting there watching them, but to my relief, he shut the door without a second glance.

Why should he worry, after all?

They were everything they should've been—young and beautiful. A perfect, happy family.

There was only one problem.

Amma was a liar, and I was going to prove it.

CHAPTER EIGHT

Somehow, finding out Amma had a family too made me feel a bit better. It meant I wasn't the only one getting made a fool of. Though I took no pleasure in knowing I was going to tear a family apart, I was relieved to know I wasn't the only victim in this messed-up situation.

Maybe that made me a monster. I wasn't sure.

All I knew was that I found myself driving home with a bit of pep in my step.

I found Joe in the kitchen, sitting at the table with the calendar and a stack of bills as he sorted through them. "Hey," I said when he didn't seem to notice me.

He hardly glanced up, his eyes distant. Focused on the task at hand. "Hey."

I moved to the sink and washed my hands before opening the freezer and pulling out a frozen lasagna.

He scribbled something on the counter. "Did you remember to pay the water bill?"

"Yeah, it's crossed out, isn't it?"

"No." He marked through it with unnecessary force.

"Oh. Sorry. I must've forgotten."

He didn't respond to that, his brows drawn down, jaw tight. "What about the phone bill?"

"Paid."

He groaned, banging his fist on the table. "Damnit, Edith. You've got to remember to mark this stuff off."

"I said I was sorry, didn't I? I guess I forgot. What's the big deal? It's not like I ever forget to pay it."

"How would I know that if you don't mark them out?"

I pressed the button to preheat the oven to the temperature listed on the box, then set it down on the counter. "Well, maybe we should get something bigger, like a whiteboard? I always forget to look at the calendar."

"Maybe you should just stop forgetting," he grumbled.

I spun around, shocked by the harshness of his tone. "Why are you in such a bad mood?"

His brows loosened instantly, the tension disappearing from his jaw. "Sorry. I'm not. This is just all a mess. We got another bill from your ultrasound. Six hundred dollars." He waved the paper in the air.

"What?" The air was sucked from the room, my

stomach churning with the news. "Six hundred? That can't be right. Insurance was supposed to cover it." I stepped forward, taking the bill from his hands and reading over the paper. "The radiologist was out of network..."

"Yeah, so insurance didn't cover any of it."

"But...how is that possible? They can just *do* that? Just send it to a doctor out of network to read and make you pay for it without even telling you it's happening? It was ordered and performed by a doctor here. It was all supposed to be covered. For goodness' sake, it was a cancer scare! Surely they have to cover that."

He shrugged one shoulder. "I'll try to call our insurance company tomorrow, but when I called your doctor's office, they said they didn't have a radiologist on staff that day, so they had to send it out. The next closest one isn't in our network, so insurance doesn't cover that."

"Why didn't they check that before they sent it to him?"

"It's a different department."

"But...they can't just do that! We don't have six hundred dollars!" My body was cold, my palms sweaty. "The electric bill's gone up thanks to the cold front, and the car payment is already behind."

Sensing my discomfort, he put a hand on my hip. "It's fine. We'll figure it out. As long as we're making payments, they won't send it to collections."

I sighed, wanting to say more, but the oven beeped

and interrupted my train of thought. His hand dropped as I backed away and crossed the room to slide the lasagna in the oven.

"We'll figure it out. We always do." Behind me, I heard the sound of the chair scooting against the tile floor, and his footsteps headed in my direction. His hands slipped around my waist, and he rested his chin on my shoulder.

I put my head down, my hand gripping the counter as the unexpected tears burned my eyes. I stifled a sob as my shoulders began to shake.

"Are you crying? What's wrong?" He tugged me toward him. "What is it? Is this about the bill or..."

"It's not about the bill. Or maybe it is. I don't know. I'm just so sick of always *figuring it out.*" I pinched the bridge of my nose, battling back tears. "I'm so sick of everything."

"What are you talking about?"

I turned around, shrugging him off. "I just don't understand how we got here, Joe."

"Here?"

"Here." I gestured around the room, around our life. "When did life become so hard? I feel like we're constantly going back and forth from one terrible thing to the next. I'm so exhausted." My last statement came out as a whisper as if I were too exhausted to even say it.

"I know." He tried to pull me into a hug, but I busied myself by picking up a hand towel from the countertop and folding it carefully. I swiped a tear from my cheek with the back of my hand and laid the towel down.

"I'm going to take a shower."

"Want me to join you?" he offered.

"No. I won't be long." I stepped out of the kitchen before he could say anything else and headed down the hall. Not taking the hint, he followed closely behind. When I reached the door, I turned around, moving to shut the door and feigning shock when I saw him behind me. "What are you doing?"

"I *want* to join you..." His eyes softened as he cocked his head to the side, willing me to accept.

"You don't have to."

"I know. I want to." He stepped forward, moving past me and pulling his shirt over his head. My husband was in impeccable shape. Once, I'd found it impossible to take my eyes off of him when he undressed. Now, I couldn't be bothered to look.

"I'm just taking a quick shower, Joe, really."

He glanced over his shoulder at me, pausing. "Is there a reason you don't want me to shower with you?"

I took a step back. "I didn't say I don't want you to."

His brows knitted together with frustration, his shoulders suddenly stiff. "You don't have to say it. You're showing it. Is this because of the pictures? Because of the app?"

I hesitated, trying to decide how I wanted to handle the conversation. My eyes darted away from his, and I ran my finger across the wall absentmind-edly. "I just feel self-conscious around you right now."

"What are you talking about?" he asked, running a hand through his chestnut hair in disbelief.

"You've obviously been looking at pictures of a woman who looks nothing like me. How do you think that makes me feel?"

He pressed a finger to his temple, his forehead wrinkling. His eyes blazed with a rage-filled fire, and when he spoke, he was obviously restraining himself. "We've been over this. I-I've told you that wasn't me. I don't know how to make that more clear to you."

"I know what you told me, but you offered no other reasonable explanation."

"I told you it was Sam."

"You told me it could've been Sam. Did you ever ask Sam about it?"

He scoffed, his cheeks flushing scarlet. "No. I haven't had a chance to... It's not exactly the easiest thing to bring up, you know? Imagine if he didn't do it, then how would I look? And, anyway, you know I wouldn't cheat on you. What happened before—it was a mistake, but I've more than made up for it. It won't happen again. You have to trust me."

"I want to," I admitted, my voice trembling. "But how can I, when I find stuff like that? And like the dating app. That's suspicious. You have to admit that it is. How would you feel if the situation were reversed?"

"I don't care how it looks. I care about what I'm telling you and whether you do or don't trust me..."

I hesitated, not processing the question in his words as my mind swam with confusion and frustration. As soon as I'd realized, I knew it was too late. His face puckered with anger as he sucked in a sharp breath.

"You know what?" He reached in his pocket and pulled out his phone, tossing it to me with force. It landed with a *crack* on the floor. "Why don't you just keep the thing if you're so worried about it? Jesus, there's no winning with you."

"I don't want to—"

He bent down, picking up his shirt and storming past me. I flinched as he slammed the door behind him without another word. Glancing down at the phone on the ground, my throat went dry.

This wasn't what I wanted... Was it?

I tapped in the password he used for everything, and my stomach sank.

It was all gone—the pictures of Amma, the dating app, all of his text messages, everything.

His social media apps had been deleted.

His email app was gone.

The phone had practically been wiped clean.

Maybe it was meant to make me feel safe, but as I stared at the blank screen, I couldn't help thinking this was further proof he had something to hide.

CHAPTER NINE

When Joe fell asleep that night, I slipped out of bed and made my way back into the living room. It was funny, really. All his lying had made it so I had to be the one to sneak around.

I unplugged my laptop from where it charged on the coffee table and sank down on the couch, pulling up our county's property records website. I recalled the house number and the street name where Amma lived and typed it into the search box, holding my breath as it pulled up results.

I released my breath when a name pulled up. Not Amma, but a man. Obviously, the man I'd seen. Her husband.

Phillip Ashton.

I opened a new tab, searching for his name. The top result was his social media account.

Finally, I was getting somewhere. Finally, there'd been a break in the case.

When this was over, maybe I'd look into becoming a detective.

Or, maybe I'd just binge hours of *SVU* and feel superior when I figured something out before they did.

Phillip's profile picture was one of him holding the young girl I'd seen today. She was younger in the photo, not quite as much blonde hair as what she had now. His profile was locked, making it nearly impossible to find out anything about him.

When I clicked on his photo, there were only four comments.

June Costello: What a cutie!

Phillip Ashton: Thanks. You're not so bad yourself, June.

June Costello: LOL! I'll tell Henry he's got some competition. Zoe's looking more and more like her momma every day. Give her kisses from me. Give Amma kisses too! Love you kids. Come home soon and see us.

Phillip Ashton: Yep, she got all of Amma's looks, thank goodness. We love you too. We'll be back before you know it.

The conversation ended there, but finally, I had a name for her. Amma Ashton. I opened another tab and searched for her. The results were useless—the only Amma Ashton pulling up had been born in 1930.

You look great for your age, Amma.

Social media was a bust, too...

Who in the world doesn't have social media these days?

The sound of Joe coughing in the bedroom made me clear my browser history, close out of the browsers and tuck the laptop away. I waited a few minutes before tiptoeing back down the hall, a bottle of water in hand, in case I needed a reason for being out of bed.

I still didn't have answers, but I was closer. I had a puzzle piece, and I'd locked it into place.

CHAPTER TEN

I awoke the next morning with a start, realizing Joe was gone. In his place in bed, there was a note.

Pack a bag.
We're going to go away for a while.
I want to remind you of who we used to be.

I read the note, utterly perplexed. We couldn't afford to go anywhere. We couldn't even afford to stay where we were, honestly. I picked up my phone on the nightstand and dialed his number, wiping sleep from my eyes as I waited for him to answer.

As I heard the familiar buzzing from his side of the bed, the events of the night before came rushing back to me. He'd left his phone with me. So, where was he?

Where had he gone?

I ended the call, ending the buzzing, and rolled

across the bed to pick up his phone. When I did, the door to the bedroom opened, and Joe appeared. His nose was as red as his coat, snowflakes gathered in his dark hair. He smiled at me, pulling the thick gloves off his hands as he set down the white plastic sacks.

"Morning, sleepyhead."

"What are you doing?" I eased myself up in bed, resting against the headboard.

"I'm taking you on a trip."

"But, you have work."

"I'm taking a few days off."

"*I* have work."

"You're taking a few days off, too. We're both very ill." He smirked.

I couldn't bring myself to return the wry grin. I sighed, running a hand over my forehead. "Joe, we can't afford it. And, even if we could, we can't just ignore our responsibilities."

He lifted his knee, sinking onto the foot of the bed and crawling toward me, his chin jutted forward. "We have a responsibility to our own happiness, too, don't you think?" When he reached me, his lips pressed to mine, and their ice-cold touch shocked me. "I'd sooner lose everything than lose you, Edie."

It was a nickname I'd never been particularly fond of. One he very rarely used. I felt something deep in my stomach flinch at the sound of it and wondered if he'd noticed.

I sighed, crossing my arms over my lap. "Well,

where are we going, then? Where's this magical destination?"

"You'll see." He patted my leg, his grip firm on my thigh as he slid off the bed. "Come on, now. Call in to work, get your bag packed, and let's hit the road." He retrieved his suitcase from the top of our closet and began loading it with items from the grocery bags—toiletries and snacks, mostly.

I lifted the covers from my legs, my body stiff from sleep. "How many outfits should I pack?"

"Just a night's worth. Although you may want to pack an extra outfit just in case."

"Just in case?" I didn't like the sound of that.

"In case we get stuck there. There's a blizzard coming."

"A blizzard?"

He nodded toward the window, and I stepped in front of it, pulling the curtains to the side. Frost gathered on the glass, and the bare trees swayed to and fro in the wind. I shivered as cool air entered through the gaps next to our windows and the thin panes of glass, grazing my arms.

"How much are they predicting?"

"Oh, you know how it is in the South. Anywhere from one to eighty-seven inches. But even a half inch will shut the town down."

I couldn't help the smile that curved my lips then. He wasn't wrong. "Do you think it's a good idea to travel in it?"

"Oh, yeah. We'll be fine. You forget I'm from Cleveland. We actually know how to drive in the snow up there."

"Yeah, but these roads aren't like Cleveland roads."

"I know that. Which is why we'll leave before it gets here. The storm is moving fast, and it should be over by early morning, like three-ish, so that'll give them plenty of time to clear the major roads. They're already salting them now. And if it gets worse than expected, we'll just stay an extra day." He beamed. "See, I've got it all figured out."

"What if we get snowed in?"

He was quiet for a moment, and I jolted when I felt his cold hands slide under my shirt. I hadn't heard him coming up behind me. When he spoke, his voice was a low growl in my ear. "I'll keep you warm."

I forced a smile, though he couldn't see my face, and I stiffened as I felt his lips on my neck, his breath warm on my cool skin. "Come on. I think we need this. I... I don't want to fight with you anymore. I want us to be okay."

"I want that, too," I admitted. His hands slipped lower on my stomach, his fingers sliding under the waistband of my pants. He kissed my shoulder, my neck, my hair. When he removed his hands, he spun me around, pressing me against the icy window.

"I love you."

"I love you, too." I couldn't meet his eye as I said it, the sting of the words raw in my chest. Even telling the truth was painful. I didn't *want* to love him anymore. I didn't want to trust him. I wanted to be able to walk away, to shut my emotions down and pretend like nothing had happened between us, but I wasn't that woman. I cared too much, loved him too deeply.

Packing seemed to be forgotten as he pulled me closer to him, sliding my shirt over my head as his kisses trailed down my chest. He led us to the bed, next to the now-empty bags from the store, and gently laid me on the knot of our tangled comforter.

"There'll be more of this when we get there," he said, his voice deep and seductive. Try as I might, I couldn't bring myself to go there. I couldn't even shut down and enjoy it, as badly as I wanted to. I tensed as he moved farther down my stomach, standing up at once and practically shoving him off me.

"What the hell—" He stood to face me.

"Sorry. I have to pee. And we should probably get ready...if we're going to beat the storm."

He watched me as I walked away but didn't protest. He was angry, but he wouldn't say so. He was too busy trying to prove we were okay to start a fight, even when he wanted to.

That was where I had the upper hand.

CHAPTER ELEVEN

F our hours later, we pulled into the parking lot of a hotel a town over. The snow had begun—still mostly flurries, the white flakes dancing on the wind and scattering across the dark pavement.

I wanted to ask how we could afford to stay at such a nice place—nice by my standards anyway, especially on an unnecessary splurge—but I didn't. I couldn't bring myself to jinx it.

Just add it to the mounting credit card debt.

In truth, I did need a vacation, and this was the closest we'd get. Even though it was a terrible idea, I deserved to be treated. I deserved to have him dote on me for a change.

And *dote*, he did. He was on his best behavior, better than I'd probably ever seen him. It was made obvious pretty quickly that while on this trip, I wasn't expected, or even allowed, to lift a finger.

With the car shut off, he unbuckled and stepped out of his side, dashing around the car to open my door before I had the chance. He held the door open for me, waiting until I was out of the car and bundled in my coat before grabbing both suitcases and dragging them behind him on our way into the hotel lobby.

"Come on, let's get inside in the warmth," he said, pretending to race me.

The place was bright, white, and sterile—almost like we were in a hospital. We checked in and retrieved our room keys, following the signs that led down the hall and toward the elevators.

Once we were inside the elevators, I looked over at him, so bundled in his coat he was hardly recognizable. "Thank you."

His eyes widened when he looked at me, and it was as if it took a moment for him to process what I'd said. "For what?"

I closed my eyes, trying to soak up the moment. "Bringing me here. This was exactly what I needed."

When I opened my eyes, he studied me for half a second, then gave a slow nod. "Yeah, I think we both did."

The elevator dinged overhead, and the doors slid open, revealing the empty hallway. We stepped out and turned left, following the signs that directed us to our room.

Once we'd reached it, he held open the door for me again, still struggling with the bags.

"I can help you, you know."

"I know you can," he assured me. "But I don't want you to." He placed our bags on the end of the bed with a loud sigh, still catching his breath as I began removing my many layers of outerwear.

The room was small but clean, with a king-size bed against the wall and a large-screen TV directly across from it. I laid my coat, gloves, and hat on the simple, wooden credenza that held the TV, ignoring the vague scent of stale cigarette smoke and cleaning products.

Joe pulled a bottle of wine from his luggage and wiggled it in the air. "Want a drink?"

I glanced at the clock. "It's hardly noon."

"So? We're on vacation." He picked up a small paper cup next to the coffeepot and unwrapped it, filling it to the brim with the cheap, white wine. Without waiting for me to accept his offer, he filled the second cup and passed it my way. "Here's to us."

"To us," I murmured, tapping my cup to his and taking a sip before setting it down on the table next to the bed. I paced the room, my arms wrapped around myself as I took in our new environment.

I parted the curtains, checking how many cars were outside. It was a quiet town that was far from a tourist destination, and from the looks of the parking lot, there were only a few other guests.

Why did you choose this place, Joe?

I didn't dare ask it. Didn't dare jinx the situation, but I couldn't deny the worry in my gut. It was ever present these days. He kicked back on the bed, one hand behind his head as he sipped his wine and watched me. "I know it's not exactly the nicest place, but—"

"It's perfect," I said, cutting him off. "Absolutely perfect."

"Yeah?" His brows rose with pure joy.

"Yeah." I closed the curtains, moving toward him and climbing into bed. I rested my head on his chest, listening to the erratic *thump-thump, thump-thump, thump-thump* that told me he was just as nervous as I felt.

"I'm really glad we could do this. I know I always say I'm going to take you somewhere, and between work and money...it's always just too much. But you deserve trips like this, Edith. You do. I wanted to make sure you knew that. I'm going to get better about showing you how much I appreciate you, okay?"

I swiped my sweaty palm across the comforter, looking up at him. "Okay." It was all I could muster up the courage to say, even if it was lame.

On paper, he was saying all the right things. I wanted so badly for that to be enough.

He met my eyes, his lips parting slightly—a question in his gaze. He slid down next to me, moving slowly and in complete silence, his eyes locked with mine. When we lay face-to-face, he cupped my cheek with his hand. His dark eyes danced between mine, and he brushed my nose with his.

He smiled, filling me with nervous butterflies like he always had. He leaned forward, giving me a chance to stop him before pressing his lips to mine gently. He pulled back, our lips a mere space apart as he waited for me to meet him the rest of the way.

"Kiss me..." he begged.

My breathing caught, and my stomach knotted as I leaned toward him, giving in and kissing him deeper. I squeezed my eyes shut, ignoring the sudden tears that burned them as our kiss grew.

Who else have you kissed this way, Joe?

Who else have you touched?

Who else have you shared a bed with?

He rolled me over gently, his body pressing down on me. Suddenly, I couldn't get enough air. My throat was tight, my heart rate accelerating. I couldn't breathe. I was being crushed. He was going to kill me. I couldn't breathe.

Couldn't catch my breath.

Couldn't move.

I was pinned.

Trapped.

"*Joe, stop—*" I practically screamed, trying to catch my breath and shove his face away from mine with both hands. He froze, then scrambled to get off of me.

"*What?* What is it? What's wrong?" His hands surrounded my face, not quite landing on my skin as he surveyed me, checking the space around us. "You're all red. What happened? Did I hurt you? How could I have hurt you?"

"I can't breathe. Something's wrong. I can't..." But even as I said it, my breathing was coming back to me. I no longer felt like I was suffocating. No longer pinned. No longer trapped.

He'd hardly put any weight on me. He wasn't trying to hurt me.

What was happening to me?

I'd never felt anything like it.

The tears in my eyes fell to my cheeks. I swallowed rapidly, my cheeks hot with embarrassment. "I'm..."

Who was I? I couldn't even bring myself to kiss my husband anymore without breaking down. How would I ever pull this off? Even when I wanted to kiss him, my body betrayed me.

A realization swept over his expression, and I watched it harden. A grimace lingered on his face. "You can't even kiss me anymore, can you? Can't even bring yourself to touch me. All because of some wild idea you've cooked up." He took an uneasy step backward, shaking his head and turning away from me. "I brought you here. Spent money we don't really have. I gave you my phone. Deleted my social media. What more do you want from me, Edith? What more can I do? How long will I have to pay for one mistake that I made a year ago? Do you just want to keep punishing me? Is it fun for you?"

"Of course it's not fun for me." The pain in his eyes

stung. Maybe even more than the words. "I stayed with you because I wanted to be with you. Because I love you."

"And things were great! We worked it out. So why have things suddenly changed?"

I pressed my lips together, frustrated that things had come to this point again. How convenient that he kept sweeping these very real issues under the rug. Then again, maybe I was guilty of the same thing. "Because of the pictures! And the app—"

"Oh my god, if we have to talk about these pictures one more time. I'm telling you, I have no idea how they got on my phone. I have no idea why the app was back on my phone. I swear to you I don't. But I've deleted them. And now you have my phone—"

"That's not what I want—"

"What *do* you want? For the love of God, please, Edith, please tell me what it is that you want. Because nothing I do seems to be enough."

I hung my head, picking at a piece of lint on my shirt. After a moment, I said, "I just want to trust you again, and I don't know what that will take." I swallowed, fighting back tears. "I don't know if I can."

He sucked in a breath, then released it slowly, taking a half step backward. His hands closed into fists, then opened wide, fingers splayed again. When he spoke, his voice was calm, despite his stiff stance. "And where does that leave us?" With that question, he had tears in his eyes that matched my own.

I shook my head, my limbs tingling with fatigue. "I wish I knew."

His lips pinched together until they rolled inward. His hands lifted and fell at his sides in a half shrug. "Okay. I'm not really sure what else to say."

"I want this trip to be the start of fixing us. I really do want that, Joe."

He shook his head, looking around. "I thought we were already fixed. Stupid me, right?"

"You're not stupid." I reached for his arm as he tried to move past me.

"Apparently, I am."

"Joe—"

"*I can't even touch you.*" He held out his hands, lifting them as if he were going to touch my cheeks, but stopping centimeters before our skin connected, so close I could feel his warmth. "Can't even kiss you without you having a full-blown panic attack. It was one mistake. *One.*" He held up a finger. "A year ago. I've apologized. I've cut off contact with her. I've done everything you asked me to do. And I've never done anything to hurt you since. The pictures, the app... I don't know what to say. I realize how bad it looks, but I've told you all I can tell you. I've been honest with you. I think the app was from an update, but I have no way to prove that, and I've never seen those pictures before in my life. I can't explain them, but I can tell you they aren't mine. I was either hacked, or Sam put them on there. I don't know." He paused, collecting himself. "Edith, I'm... I'm telling you the truth. I'd never be that stupid again. And if you won't believe me, I'm not sure how else to prove that to you."

I sank down onto the bed, my hands in my lap. "I wish I knew. I really do. I wish I knew the magic formula to make this all better."

"Just tell me what to do, and I'll do it—"

"That's just it." I cut him off, putting my hands on his chest as he moved toward me. "I'm not so sure there's anything you *can* do."

"So, what? We're just...done? Do you want a divorce? Is that what you're telling me?"

My blood ran cold. "I don't know what I want. I just...I think I need time."

"But I've done nothing wrong!" he shouted, his eyes bulging.

"I understand that. But whether or not there's an explanation, the pictures, and the app were on your phone. It's a hell of a coincidence. Maybe you were hacked. Maybe Sam put them there. But we don't know that. And it's bringing back all the old feelings from the last time I caught you. Because you *have* done this before, Joe. And I know you've made it up to me, and I know you've worked hard to fix it and apologize, but this is all reminiscent of that. And I can't help the way I feel right now." I stood, squaring my shoulders to him. "Maybe this is the vacation we need. But you have to be as patient and understanding with me as you're asking me to be with you."

The sound of a soft vibration interrupted him just as he opened his mouth to argue. He closed it again, walking over to his coat and pulling out his phone. It hadn't taken him long to admit he wanted the device back. He glanced up at me. "It's my mom." Then, with a hint of irritation in his expression, he flipped the phone around so I could indeed see her name on the screen. He placed the phone to his ear. "Hello?" He paused, then his brows drew down. "Wait, what? When?" He sighed, reaching for his coat. "No, wait. Just..." He glanced around the room, then snatched the keys from the nightstand. "Just hang on, okay? Will you wait for me? I'll be there in an hour. It's not safe, okay? You just...stay there. Stay in the car until I get there, and we'll figure this out." He ended the call, cursing under his breath as he pulled his coat and scarf on.

"What's going on?" I reached for my own coat, a new fear filling me.

He blinked, completely distracted as if he'd forgotten I was still there. "It's... It's Mom. She's out somewhere, apparently without Dad. She can't figure out where she is, and she's crying and talking about walking to find help. I've gotta call him. I've gotta call the police." He shoved his phone in his pocket, then pulled it back out, spinning in circles as he searched for the keys already in his hand.

"Wait. You can't go out in the storm. Where's your dad?"

"I don't know. Where did I put my hat?"

I reached for his arm, but he pulled away.

"Wait, Joe, you can't go alone. Let me get my things—"

Brought back to reality, he shook his head, his expression stony. "No. I'm not taking you out in this." He held out a hand, forcing me to stop in my tracks. "I'll be back. You wait here."

"It's not safe for you to go alone."

"Have you seen my hat?" He spun around again.

I grabbed his hat from beside the TV and passed it to him. "I should go. I can help you look for her."

"I'll be fine. I don't have a choice." He took the hat, then started to walk away. Suddenly, he stopped, turning back, his eyes searching mine. "I love you. I *will* be back." He leaned forward gently, aiming for my mouth, then seemed to think better of it and landed on my cheek.

"I love you, too. Please be careful."

He nodded, searching for his keys again—still in his hand—patting his pocket to be sure his phone was there, and tugging on his hat.

Then, in a flash, he was gone. The door shut with a loud thud behind him, leaving me bitterly alone in the silence, replaying everything that had just happened as the storm raged on outside.

CHAPTER TWELVE

"Hello, and thank you for calling the my-husband-is-a-scumbag hotline. Dan speaking. How may I direct your call?" His singsong voice came over the line.

"He brought me to a hotel in Dakota."

"What?"

"I'm in a hotel. Alone. In a blizzard."

"Well, blizzard is a bit of a stretch, but—"

"Dan!"

He cleared his throat. "Sorry, let me try that again. *What on earth? Why?*"

"I have no idea. We came here to get away and try to fix things, and then his mom called, and he had to go there. So now I'm just sitting here alone, waiting."

He cleared his throat, apparently rendered speechless. "You mean to tell me this man took you to a hotel in the middle of a blizzard—the size of which I will not get into—and then left you there alone, still in the middle of said blizzard?"

"Yup." I drained the last of the wine from my cup.

"Mmmkay. And how are you handling that?"

"I'm sitting on the bed, drinking wine from a paper coffee cup, and calling you."

He inhaled. "Okay, sweetie. Listen up. Now is not the time to wallow. Your husband is cheating on you. He ditches you most nights of the week. Now, he's left you in a hotel alone. What more is it going to take?"

"I'm working up the nerve..." I admitted.

"The nerve to what? Leave him? Because I will help you find that nerve. Let me come get you. You can stay with me until you're back on your feet. I'll have Nick and his friends go get your stuff. We can just sit here and look pretty and let them do all the work."

I sighed, dreaming of the possibility. "You know it's not that simple."

"Why the hell isn't it?"

"We're married. I can't just break up with him. All of our stuff is combined. Our bills. Our finances. Our things. If I'm going to leave him, I have to be woman enough to tell him the truth."

"Like *he* was man enough to tell *you* the truth, you mean?"

"He's still denying it," I squeaked.

"Still denying what?"

"The pictures. He says he was hacked. I also found a dating app on his phone that he said was old."

"You didn't!"

"I did. Last night. He said it must've come back with an old update."

"Where does he get these lines? How to be a lying asshole dot com?" He groaned loudly. "Look, do you need me to go on this app and find him? 'Cause I'll do it? I'll create a fake profile and Candy Apple Carmen my way all up in his DMs."

"Candy Apple Carmen?" I snorted.

"It would be my fake dating app name. Something disgustingly sweet. Or...Alexis Sunflower. Bambi Bonita."

"Those sound...incredibly fake."

"Everyone's fake on those things, girl. Haven't you ever been on one?"

"Well, no, actually."

He laughed. "Okay, well, my humor is entirely lost on you. Anyway, I wouldn't go *quite* that obvious, but I can find out if he's cheating if you want me to make a fake account."

"No, it's okay. I appreciate the offer, but that's why we're here. He's trying to fix this, or whatever."

"Honey, it's going to take more than some cheap wine in a motel to fix this. I hope you told him that."

"I did. So now he's deleted all his social media, the dating app, and all his photos. He basically wiped his phone clean and said I can keep it."

"He gave you his phone?"

"I mean, I gave it back! I'm not trying to control him, and I do think he's trying to fix this, but—"

He gasped. "*Trying to fix this?!* Please! Bitch has got another phone, girl. Can't you see that?"

A stone dropped in my stomach. It hadn't even occurred to me. "No... You don't think he really does, do you? How could he? I would've noticed."

"Of course, I think that. No one in the year 2022 gives up their phone and goes on with their lives unless they're a celebrity doing it for like two hours for attention. Get real. And how would you have noticed? Are you checking his things? His car? Maybe he keeps it at work."

"No..."

"What about your bank accounts? Are you checking them? Because you didn't even know about the other women until it was staring you in the face." Dan's version of tough love was exceptionally tough at times, but I truly knew it came from a good place. He'd protected me so often—from me, from others. I knew I could count on him to be honest with me, even when I didn't want to hear it.

"I haven't checked them, no. But there's hardly any money in the accounts. We couldn't afford a secret phone bill."

"You'd be surprised what people can afford when they're desperate. Besides that, why are you struggling so badly? I mean, we've always been boxed-wine girls, but you've never struggled as much as since you married Joe. And you're still living in your apartment, so your bills haven't changed. You've just added his income. If anything, you should be doing better."

"Joe's got student loans. He helps out his parents. Plus, there's a whole extra person living in my apartment, using water and electricity, and food. My bills have definitely gone up."

He let out a quick breath. "Well, how long do you have? You should pull up your accounts and sort through them. Flag anything that looks strange."

"I check my account all the time." *Every time I need to buy something.*

"*Your* account? Wait... Wait... Wait..." He drew in a long inhale. "You mean you don't *share* accounts? Why is this the first I'm hearing of this?"

"Oh, come on. Would you like to join us in the twenty-first century? Women aren't property anymore. We don't have to share bank accounts. That was never important to me. We split the bills and responsibilities. As long as his half is paid, I don't care what he spends his money on, and he feels the same way about me."

"Except *you* have no money, honey. How do you know he doesn't?"

The floor had been pulled out from under me. Even as I fought to find my footing, I was realizing my many mistakes. "Because... Because he's told me he doesn't."

"And we all know he's just a pillar of honesty." He

clapped his hands together. "Do you at least have access to his accounts? Do you have the passwords?"

"They're...written down somewhere." We'd written them down for emergencies in a notebook that was stored in his desk at home. At the time, it hadn't seemed that important. I never thought Joe would lie to me.

"Okay, do you know where?"

"At home."

"And Joe's not at home, right?"

"No. He's somewhere out looking for his mom."

"How long do you think we have before he comes back and realizes you're gone?"

"What do you mean?"

"I'm coming to get you. We're going to go home and look for the passwords and you're going to look through your husband's bank account to see what he's hiding."

I crossed one leg over the other, tucking a hand under my thigh. "And what if he's not hiding anything?"

"Then at least you'll know that for a fact." He didn't sound convinced.

"I can't let you get out in this storm."

"*Let?*" He scoffed, tossing my joke back to me. "Want to join us in the twenty-first century? And I'll have you know, I'm an excellent driver in the snow."

"You literally wrecked your car last year while driving in the snow."

"Excuse me, that was ice. Anyway, who else do you have? Hm?" He was teasing then, but it was painfully true. There was no one else I could call. No one that I trusted like I trusted Dan.

"I don't want you to get hurt."

"That's exactly why we have to do this." His tone was serious then, and I swallowed, sitting up on the bed. "We have to find out the truth because *I* can't let anyone hurt *you*, but especially not him. He didn't deserve you last time, and he certainly doesn't deserve you this time."

"Okay," I said finally, unable to fight my own curiosity any longer. "If you're sure you can drive in this."

"I'll make it. Can you text me the address?"

"As soon as we're off the phone. Be safe, okay?"

"Yep, love you. See you in just a bit."

As we ended the call, true fear began to set in over what we might find. What if Joe was lying to me about more than an affair? How would I handle it?

I scrolled through the phone, searching for Joe's name in my call log. When I found it, I placed the phone to my ear and waited. On the third ring, he answered, "Hello?"

"Hey, did you find her?"

"Not yet. It's not exactly easy in this mess." There was a bite to his tone, and I sensed he was concentrating on something. In the background, I could hear the sound of the windshield wipers working at their highest speed.

"Have you talked to your dad?"

"Yeah, he was in the shower. He had no idea she'd taken the car. The doors were all locked, and he thought she was asleep."

"Oh no." I inhaled sharply, swallowing down my guilt. "So now what? Did you call the police?"

"Yeah, the police know. We're all out looking for her. Luckily, the car has a GPS tracker, so it won't be hard to loc—" He paused. "Hey, I've gotta go. The police are calling me."

"Okay, call me back when you—"

The call ended, and he was gone, but I'd found out what I needed to. I hoped his mom was found safe. But, for now, I knew he'd be busy for at least the next few hours. If we hurried, Dan and I could make it home and back without getting caught.

CHAPTER THIRTEEN

As much as I'd thought the plan could work, an hour later, Dan still hadn't arrived. I was trying not to be impatient as I waited, pacing and watching out the window with nerves flitting through my stomach. When my phone rang, my breathing quickened. Spying his name on the screen brought me only a tiny bit of relief.

What if he was hurt?

What if something happened?

"Hello?"

"I'm coming into town now," he said, his voice filled with determination.

My shoulders rose with a long inhale, and I spoke as I exhaled. "Okay, thank god. I'll stand outside the entrance."

"Be careful. It's blizzarding out here," he teased.

I turned to walk out of the room, ending the call

but froze when I heard a noise outside the door. A second later, the hotel room door opened and a confused-looking Joe stood in front of me. His gaze raked over me, his expression wrinkling.

"Were you going somewhere?"

"You're back!" My body trembled with adrenaline as I tried to come up with an explanation that made sense. Funny how the roles had been reversed. "Um, I was going to walk across the road and get something to eat." I rubbed my belly, just then realizing how hungry I actually was.

He was still for a moment, then nodded. "Oh, okay." He glanced at his watch, then his phone. "Shoot. Yeah. I'm sorry. I didn't even think about getting you something to eat before I left."

Of course he didn't. He left in a hurry. It was an emergency.

Why wasn't he telling me what happened?

How had he made it back so quickly?

"Did you find your mom? Is she okay?"

"Oh, yeah. She's fine," he said, shoving his hands in his pockets. "They're having the car towed, and Dad is bringing her back home safe and sound. She'd pulled over on the interstate, and luckily, a cop had stopped to help her. When he called it in, they called me, so I just turned around."

"She must've been so scared..." Like I was right then.

"She seems okay. Rattled and confused but glad to

be with my dad again. We're just lucky she still remembers us...even if she's forgotten so much else." There was a heavy sadness in his eyes then that made me want to pull him into a hug. But I couldn't—I was too busy panicking. "Anyway, I'm sorry I had to leave so suddenly." He pointed toward the door. "Should we go get something to eat, then?"

"I, um..." I chewed my lip. "Yeah, just one second. I need to use the restroom before we go." I stepped to my left, into the bathroom, and shut the door behind me, pulling out my phone as quickly as I could.

I opened my last text to Dan and typed out a new message as quickly as possible.

He's back. He's in the room. Go back home. We'll have to do this another time. I'm so sorry.

I flushed the toilet for good measure while I waited for a response, which wasn't coming. There was a knock on the bathroom door.

"Uhh... You okay in there?"

I turned on the water. "Fine. I'll be right out."

Come on, Dan.

Come on. Come on. Come on.

Finally, a message came through.

Do you still keep a spare key above the doorframe?

I sucked in a breath. If Joe knew about the key, he'd call me ridiculous. Or potentially unsafe. But I'd have to add this to the long list of times I was glad it was there. **Yes.**

There was another knock on the bathroom door as I read his message.

Be careful. I'll let you know what I find.

"What's going on, Edith?" Joe rattled the door handle.

I shoved my phone in my pocket, washing my hands rapidly and swinging the door open. "Jeez, calm down. I'm sorry. That wine ran straight through me."

I wasn't sure he believed me, but there was no time for further discussion. I led the way through the door and down the hall, forcing a quivering smile as we stepped into the elevator. "Is it getting bad out there yet?"

He cocked his head to the side. "Not awful, but it's quite a storm. Worse than they expected, I think."

I could've sworn I saw the edge of his mouth twitch into a smile.

Did he know I was lying to him? Did he know something was up?

I forced a smile of my own. *Quite a storm indeed.*

CHAPTER FOURTEEN

W e walked across the parking lot slowly, fighting against the blistering wind and cold on our way to the small restaurant across the street.

When we reached it, I half wondered if I should've asked Dan to stay. If I should've jumped into his car and demanded he drive off the second I was safely inside. But that was ridiculous, wasn't it?

For all the things my husband was, he wasn't dangerous. He couldn't be.

As we made it inside the restaurant, the bell above the door chimed to announce our welcome, and a plump man behind the counter looked up from the book in his hand.

He chuckled to himself, setting the book down. "Well, alright. I didn't think anyone would be out in this."

"Yeah, not the smartest idea we've ever had," Joe

told him, pulling the scarf from around his neck. His smile was charming. Casual. "We're, uh, we're just staying at the hotel across the street and need something to eat."

The man patted the counter. "Well, come on, then. Let's get something warm in ya."

We moved forward, my teeth chattering as I went, and took a seat in front of him. The warm, greasy scent of the diner reminded me of Jenna's, though it was notably quieter and drabber. He slid us two menus, flat and laminated, with options on both sides. Meanwhile, he filled up a cup of coffee for each of us. My hands shook as I took the steaming cup, holding it between my palms.

I wouldn't ordinarily entertain the idea of drinking black coffee, but at the moment, I was sure I would've considered lava if it meant warming the cold that had settled into my bones. Georgia winters weren't ordinarily this cold, so I never felt prepared for them.

"What brings y'all to town?"

"We live nearby," Joe answered. "We just wanted to get away for a night."

"Well, you sure picked a helluva time to do it, hm?" the man asked with another chuckle.

"Tell me about it. I'm surprised you're open, actually. I mean, obviously we're glad you are, but it seems like everything around here has already shut down," Joe told him while scanning the menu.

He moved back and forth behind the counter,

restocking the napkins and straws as he went. "Well, my boss doesn't close for much. And I don't mind it, really. Means I have somewhere to be. And I'm getting paid to stand here for the most part." When the supplies were crammed full, he approached us again, his eyes dropping down to the menu. "Made up your minds yet?"

"Could I have the tomato soup?" I asked quickly, my teeth still chattering as I rubbed my hands together. *Warmth. Please.* "With a grilled cheese?"

"And I'll take a burger with onion rings."

"Sure thing. I'll be back with ya shortly." He retrieved our menus, placing them under the counter and heading for the back of the restaurant, out of sight.

Joe removed the black beanie from his head, and snowflakes fell from it, gathering in his hair. He grinned at me, running his hand over his dark locks. "You cold? You're still shivering. Do you want my coat?"

"I'll be fine." I gripped the mug tighter. "Do you need to check in with your dad?"

"Nah," he said, taking a sip of the steaming coffee. "They'll be fine. I should let them get some rest."

"Joe, have you thought about trying to get him some help? Or...maybe trying to find a place that's big enough for the four of us to live? I know it would be even more of a stretch, but your parents wouldn't have their bills, so they could chip in a little bit. We'd make it work."

99

He took a sip of his coffee. "We've talked about trying to consolidate the four of us into a place together before and have always agreed it was a bad idea. Where is this coming from?"

"I don't know. I just... Do you think it's getting too hard with you having to go back and forth so often? I mean, it's been two years. How much longer can we do this?"

He seemed taken aback by the question. "Is it too hard for you?"

"Well, I miss you when you're gone, sure, but I wasn't asking selfishly. I just know that it must be a lot on your dad. And your mom. I know you've said change upsets her, and I know she doesn't really understand, but...maybe having you around more often would make it easier. Something permanent."

Something shifted in his gaze then. "Having *me* around more often? Not both of us?"

"Well, yes, both of us. Isn't that what I said?"

He turned his head, staring away from me with a tight jaw. "No, it's not what you said."

"Well, you know what I meant."

"I'm not sure I do." He took another drink.

I lowered my voice. "I was only trying to help. Forget I said anything, I guess."

My phone buzzed in my pocket, and I glanced around the room, searching for a sign that said—

Restrooms

There. I stood from the chair abruptly.

"I need to use the restroom again. I'll be back."

"Again?" He eyed me as I rushed away from him and toward the metal door in the back of the restaurant. Once I was inside, I stepped into a stall and locked it behind me, pulling out my phone.

"Hello?"

"Hey, you okay?"

"Yeah, I'm fine." My voice echoed in the quiet room, and I lowered it instinctually.

"Can you talk?"

"Yeah, I'm in the restroom."

"Okay, I'm in your apartment. Where is the notebook?"

"It's..." I lowered my voice further. "In the bedroom. He has a desk in the corner. I never touch it. We keep all our stuff in a green notebook."

"Okay..." I could hear his steady breathing as he moved through our apartment. I heard the creak of floors and the groan of the bedroom door as it opened. I could picture him there, knew exactly where he was by the sounds in the background. "Okay... Desk." He was shuffling papers around then, likely moving things around as he sat down. "Okay. The drawers are all locked. Do you know where he keeps the key?"

"Locked?" I swallowed, my throat suddenly too dry. "No, they shouldn't be locked."

"Well, that's unfortunate because they are. Any ideas?"

"No... I don't know." I tried to think. He'd never

mentioned locking the drawers before. "We've never locked it as far as I know, but... I guess I don't really know. I don't use the desk. We have our laptops, so it mostly just collects dust and—"

"Okay, focus," he said sharply. "Just let me think." He paused. "Okay. Let me just look around here and see... He's gotta keep the key close by."

"Okay, just be careful." I bit back the apology that was on my tongue. What would I be apologizing for? For being entirely useless? For dragging him into my drama?

I listened closely as he shuffled more stuff around, talking to himself as he moved through the small bedroom.

"Not under the lamp... Maybe in the nightstand? No, although I need to bleach my eyes now, so thanks for that." My ears burned impossibly hot. For once, I was grateful he couldn't see my face. "Okay, closet. Let's check the closet. Nothing I can't ever unsee in here, is there? No... Oh, mattress! Let me check under the mattress." He groaned. "Nope, nothing there. Under the bed?"

"Anything?"

He was out of breath when he answered. "No. I don't see it anywhere. Could it be in his car, maybe?"

"Maybe, but we drove the car here."

"Okay." He clicked his tongue. "Well, that only really leaves us one option. Do you want me to just break into it? I'll find some tools—do you have tools? I'll find something and just go to town on this little, very unfortunate-looking desk."

"No," I said quickly. "I don't want him to know we went through it. Especially if we don't find anything."

"Did you hear me about the tools? I can make it look like someone broke in."

I wasn't sure if he was kidding or not.

"No, Dan, we have to be smart about this."

"There is no smart. There is only alive or not alive. I'm telling you, there is a reason this drawer is locked. If this psycho—" He stopped talking abruptly, the line suddenly silent.

"Dan?" I looked at the screen, checking to make sure I hadn't lost the call. "Are you there? I... I can't hear you."

When he spoke again, it was a soft whisper that sent fear ricocheting through me. "There's someone else here."

CHAPTER FIFTEEN

The hairs on the back of my neck stood on end, every nerve ending in my body on high alert. "What do you mean there's someone there? In the apartment?"

He didn't respond, though I could still hear the sounds of his steady breathing. My guess was that, whatever was happening, he couldn't respond. Whoever was in our home was too close.

For a single, fleeting moment, I considered the possibility that he might be joking, trying to trick me, but this was too real. His terrified breathing was too convincing. I was stuck between wanting to run to Joe, to demand that we go to Dan or call the police or something, and staying completely still, not wanting to let Joe in on our plan. How would I ever explain this?

Would any of that matter if something happened to Dan?

I deliberated back and forth, remaining frozen and silent as I pressed the phone to my ear harder and listened carefully to the noises on the other line.

What was happening?

Who would be in our apartment?

Were we being robbed?

Had they broken in?

Would they find him?

Would they kill him?

I couldn't bear the thought. A whimper escaped my throat, and I whispered, "Can you hear me? Should I call the police?"

His breathing was low and slow, and I heard the sound of footsteps then. I clamped a hand over my mouth, trying to keep any sounds I was making to a minimum. What if they were in the room with him? What if they heard me?

I was going to pass out.

I could feel it. My knees were weak. The room had begun to spin and blur. My chest constricted, not allowing me to inhale as deeply as I needed to. Bitter tears stung my eyes, and I squeezed them shut.

Think, Edith, think.

I shook my head, forcing away the fog, and reached for the door handle. We'd have to call the police. I had to alert Joe. Consequences be damned.

"They're gone."

I released the door handle, stepping back with a ragged breath. It was so good to hear his voice again, even shaking and filled with terror. "What? You're okay? Are you okay? Who was it? What happened?"

"I-I don't know." He sucked in sharp, panicked breaths. "I'm fine. I'm okay. I thought I heard someone at the door. I thought they'd knock and go away, but then I heard the door handle rattling. I started to step out into the hall and check out who it was, but that was when I heard the door open."

A sour taste filled my mouth. "Did they take anything? Did you see who it was?"

"I didn't see anything. I jumped under your bed like the scaredy-cat I am," he said, forcing a laugh that did nothing to cloak the fear in his voice. "Does anyone else know where you hide that key?"

"No one. Not even Joe. I forget it's there half the time." I balled up my fist, placing it to my cheek in an effort to warm my icy fingers.

"They had to have used it. I put it back above the door before I came in so I wouldn't lose it. So, either they knew where it was, they saw me putting it there, or they had a key of their own. They didn't break in, they just unlocked the door and walked in. And nothing's missing from what I can tell."

"And you're sure you locked it behind you when you came in?"

He hesitated. "I'm...yes, I mean, I'm pretty sure."

"Pretty sure?"

"Like ninety-eight and a half percent sure, okay? Either way, why would anyone have just walked in?"

I pressed my lips together, trying to think. "We've never had any trouble before... Do you think you were being followed?"

"No, not that I know of," he said thoughtfully, his voice soft. "I mean, why would I be? Who would've been following me? No one knows who I am or that I was coming by." He clicked his tongue. "Oh! Could it have been your landlord?"

"I doubt it. They have to give us notice..." I trailed off.

"Hm. Well, they got in somehow. Whoever it was."

"Someone must've seen you use the key. Either that or they picked the lock. Can you pick a dead bolt?"

"I wouldn't think so."

"Well, there are no others. No one else has a key, and no one knows where I keep that one hidden. Joe has my only other spare key. We've never made extras..." At least, *I* hadn't made extras.

"Okay, well, they're gone now. I'll be sure to lock up before I leave, but I'm getting the heck out of Dodge in case they come back. Do you want me to hide the key somewhere else to be safe?"

"Yeah, could you? Actually, would you just take it with you?" I asked, shivering. This time, the cold in my core wasn't due to the weather. "I hate to think that they might come back."

"Yeah, of course. I'll take it. But..."

"But what?"

"It's just... I was thinking. If they saw me use the

key, why wouldn't they have waited until I left if they were planning to break in? Or, on the other hand, if it was actually me that they were after, why wouldn't they have tried to actually find me? It's like they came in and left right away. Like they knew what they were coming for and didn't even know I was here."

"I don't know..." I pressed a finger to my temple, breathing slowly. "You're right. None of this makes any sense." I wanted to think maybe he'd heard a noise and mistaken it for someone coming into the apartment, but I knew that wasn't likely. My mind raced with possibilities and fear.

"Okay, the key was in the door," he said, the panic returning to his voice. "Still in the lock. I definitely didn't leave it there."

"So, whoever it was, they used it."

I heard him stretch, his voice strained. "Yep. And it's the one from on top of the door because there's no other one up here. I've got it now, though. The door is locked up tight, and I'm taking the key."

"Okay, good. Thank you." The wind whipped through the phone, a reminder that he was back out in the storm. "Please be careful. Keep an eye out around you, okay?"

"I am," he vowed. "I'm almost to my car."

"So, what happened next? After you hid under the bed? You never said."

He cleared his throat. "Nothing really. I heard

them moving around in the apartment. The kitchen or living room was as far as they could've made it. I put the phone down so I could focus on what I was hearing. I just knew they were going to come into the bedroom, so I was trying to decide whether to stay there or try to find something I could use as a weapon, but then... I heard the door shut again. And they were gone."

"Are you sure about that? You're sure they left? What if they were just hiding?"

"I'm positive." Finally, I heard the door slam, and the wind noise was cut off in an instant. "Your place isn't that big. They never came into the bedroom, and I've checked the bathroom, living room, and kitchen. Whoever it was, whatever they wanted, they're gone now."

Appreciation expanded in my chest, making me feel light headed again. How close had I come to losing my best friend? "I'm sorry I got you involved in this."

"Don't be sorry. Be safe. Do you want me to come get you? I can fake an emergency."

I thought better of it. "No, I'll be okay for the night. The storm will die down soon, and we're coming home in the morning, so just a few more hours. I'll convince him I don't feel well and go to sleep early."

"Are you sure you'll be okay?" He sounded exasperated. As if I wasn't taking the situation seriously enough. In truth, maybe I wasn't. But the more I thought about it, the more I was convinced that he'd just heard a noise from another apartment. Dan wasn't used to sharing walls with anyone, and ours were paper thin. If someone had shut their door on either side of us, he might've mistaken it for ours. That had to be it. I couldn't stand for it to be anything else.

"I'll be fine. Swear it."

"Okay. Text me every minute. Promise me. And I don't care what time it is or what the roads look like, I will drive to you the second you need me. You know that."

Suddenly, I was crying again. "I know."

"Just take care of yourself."

"I will."

"And don't believe any of his lies."

"I won't."

He sighed. "Okay, well, if I'm not coming to rescue you right now, I'm heading home. Call me if you need me, okay? And, as soon as you get home, check those accounts."

"I will," I promised him. "Thank you so much for doing this, Dan. I love you."

"I'd do it again in a heartbeat. It's why I'm here. You'd do the same for me. Love you, too."

We ended the call, and I walked out of the stall, staring at my reflection. My skin was splotchy—red in places and pale white in others. I approached the sink, washing my hands before splashing water on my face. I patted my neck with the warm water.

Just breathe.

I patted my hands, face, and neck dry, thankful to be back to seminormal. My breathing had slowed, and the panic in my expression had washed away with the warmth of the water. With a final once-over in the mirror, I pushed open the door.

At the sound of it opening, Joe eyed me suspiciously from the counter.

Our food had arrived, and mine sat steaming in front of my empty seat. My stomach rumbled at the sight.

"Everything okay?" he asked when I drew nearer to him. "You don't look so good."

"I'm, um..." My mouth watered at the sight of the food. "I'm okay. Yeah, I'm just not feeling well." I placed a hand on my stomach as I laid the pieces for my early bedtime into place. "I'm hoping this soup will calm my stomach."

"Not feeling well?" He grunted. "What, are you sick?"

"I don't know..." I eased onto the chair, wincing as I did. "I think I'll be okay. It's just a bit of a stomach bug. Probably just nerves over everything that happened earlier—between us and with your mom."

He nodded stoically. "Do you want to take this to go? We could eat up in our room so you can lie down?"

I ran my spoon over the creamy red liquid. In truth, all I really wanted was for him to stop asking questions so I could eat. Instead, I said, "That would be nice, actually. Do you mind?"

"No. Not at all. It's probably better we get back to the room before the storm picks up even more." He helped me to stand and waved over the waiter, who boxed up our dinners to go. Keeping an eye on the bag Joe put the boxes in, I was hardly listening as the two men talked, exchanging pleasantries. Once we'd paid, he led the way out of the restaurant, holding the door open for me as I passed him.

As we made our way back to the hotel, I could think of nothing other than my hunger and the events that had just occurred.

Someone had broken into my apartment.

Okay, not broken in—they'd used a key. But how did they even know about the key?

I tried to force the thought away, wanting to believe it was all a misunderstanding. No one knew where I kept that key—only Dan and me. So how had they found it? And what had they wanted in my apartment anyway? It wasn't as if I had anything worth stealing. They wanted the hand-me-down couch or my terrible credit? Be my guest.

Either way, maybe the most terrifying realization was this: Whoever they were, whatever they wanted, they'd known we'd be gone. If they hadn't followed Dan, they'd been expecting us to be away from the house. And I hadn't told anyone we'd be leaving.

Suddenly, a new thought occurred to me. Maybe the worst one of all.

Maybe Joe hadn't just wanted to take me away for a nice trip like he'd said.

Maybe this was all part of his plan.

Maybe once again, I'd fallen for his lies.

CHAPTER SIXTEEN

J oe snuggled next to me, and I breathed in the scent of him—an odd combination of fried food, a clean scent that I associated with the school though I could never quite put my finger on what it was, and his warm, woodsy cologne. It was a scent combination I was used to, one that had always made me feel safe.

I think it's important to note that, despite our problems, I did love my husband. Very much. Aside from Dan, he was the person I felt I could tell the most to. He had always had my back, taken care of me when I was under the weather, and taken my side in whatever coworker disputes I shared with him. He rubbed my feet after a long day and held my hand through my cancer scare.

When he was good, he was very, very good. I just wished that were more often.

It was hard for me to accept that the man who'd done all those things for me, the one I loved so much, was also the man who'd broken my heart. Who'd lied and snuck around and had an affair, maybe multiple affairs.

How do you deal with a revelation like that? How does anyone?

How are you just supposed to keep breathing, keep existing, keep moving on when your entire world has just splintered into a million tiny pieces, nothing seeming to fit together any longer?

"Did that soup seem to help your stomach?" he asked, interrupting my thoughts.

"A little," I said gently, nuzzling my face in his chest. For that brief moment, I found myself wishing so badly things could stay this way. That I could go back to being oblivious and believing his lies. It would've been so much easier. Not that it would have stopped him from telling them, but maybe it would've stopped the pain just a bit. "Hey, about earlier..."

He glanced over, waiting for me to go on.

"I just want you to know that I do love you. Really, truly. And I'm sorry I'm so paranoid. I still don't know what to think about that woman's photos. Or the dating app. But I know that I trust you. And if you tell me you don't know how they got there, then I'll believe you."

His expression softened, and he pressed his lips to my forehead. "I have no idea how they got there. I'd never looked at them. *Would* never look at them." He wrinkled his nose in apparent disgust. "You're all I need, sweetheart. You know that."

"I know you've made up for what happened last time and apologized over and over, but it's just...it still hurts, you know? It all still feels really raw sometimes. Especially when something like this happens. It sends me back there, no matter how much I feel like I've progressed. I'm right back in that moment, every time I think about it."

He pulled me closer to him, nodding his cheek against the top of my head. "I know. I understand. I'm sorry if I overreacted. I wasn't trying to. I just panicked when I thought I might lose you. I promised you I'd never cheat on you again when it happened last time, and I meant it. I hope you believe that."

"I have a hard time with trusting people anyway—"

"I'm not *people*, Edith. I'm your husband. I'm the man who takes care of you. Who loves you more than anything—any*one*—in this world. You're it for me. I was awful for hurting you before, and I know that now. It was a lapse in judgment, a lapse in sense. But I know better now. I'd be an absolute idiot to ever hurt you again. I like to think I'm just a little bit smarter than that."

"I just hope that, if anything were to ever happen again, that you'd be honest with me. I'd be more willing to accept another mistake if you were honest with me about it. But if I found out like I did last time, it would destroy me. Destroy us."

He chuckled. "I know you're trying to get me to admit to something here, but I swear to you, I have done nothing wrong. I'm innocent." He wiggled his brows, trailing a hand up my side. "Well, maybe not quite *innocent.*"

I gave him a nervous half smile, but looked away. "Okay. I believe you."

Without missing a beat, he kissed my forehead. "I'm glad. I love you." He placed a finger under my chin, gently urging me to look at him. When I did, his gaze was soft, his eyes full of warmth. "Hey, you can trust me, okay? I will *never* hurt you again."

I laid my head back on his chest, closing my eyes and listening to the sounds of his breathing. If I lay there for just a few more minutes, I was sure I'd fall asleep.

When my phone buzzed, I jolted from my half-asleep state and rolled over, once again the one with something to hide as I carefully checked the text from Dan.

"Everything okay?" Joe asked as I read over it.

Made it home. You okay?

"It's Dan... Oh no. Actually, I think something's wrong. I need to call him really quickly." I stood from the bed and walked toward the door, pressing the phone to my ear without actually placing the call. "Hey, what's up?"

Joe was watching me carefully from the bed.

I'd never been much of an actress, but I had to

hope the fear I truly felt would help me sell the performance. "What do you mean? Uh, no. Don't go inside, whatever you do. No, don't call the police, either. Give me just a sec. I'll call you right back." I ended the fake call and stared at my husband with a panicked expression. Did he believe me?

"The police? What's going on?" he asked, standing from the bed, obvious fear in his tone. So maybe he did.

And the Oscar goes to…

"Were you expecting anyone at our apartment?" I demanded.

He blanched. "Um, no. Why would I be?"

My shoulders fell with fake disappointment. "Well, I was hoping you were. Dan stopped by the apartment because I mentioned I wasn't feeling well earlier. I didn't tell him we were out of town, just that I thought I was coming down with something. He was out, so he picked up some soup and was going to surprise me by bringing it by. Anyway, when he got there, the door was standing open, as if someone might be inside." I put a hand to my stomach, no longer pretending to be panicking as I recalled the events. "If you weren't expecting anyone, we need to call the police." Everything hinged on the fact that he'd argue with me. If he actually agreed to call the police, this entire plan would fall apart. If he argued, it meant he'd been lying.

"Wait, no." He pressed his fingers to his temples. "Did Dan go inside?"

"No, I told him not to. If we don't know who's in there, it's not safe. I'm making him go home." I lifted my phone, pretending to tap out a message.

"Okay, good, but I just realized we don't need to call the police."

"What do you mean?"

"I totally forgot. Things have been so crazy, it's just... It's my dad," he blurted out. "I forgot that I'd told him he could stop by the house and pick up Mom's extra medication."

I wrinkled my brow, relief and anger bubbling in my belly.

Lies. Lies. Lies. Lies.

"Why was your mom's medication at our house?"

"I picked it up when I was there and forgot to leave it with them. She's not out of her meds yet, but since he was already halfway here from having to pick her up, he decided to go ahead and get them. I was going to go with him, but I was just in such a hurry to get back to you. I thought it would be fine for him to go alone."

"Oh..." I trailed off. "That seems like a lot of driving to pick up medication she didn't need yet. Couldn't you have just brought it to him when you go Friday?"

"Well, yeah, that was the plan, but she's running low, so he wanted to get them now. You're right, though, I told him it could wait, but you know how he is. I can't make either of them listen to me half the time.

It was just easier to tell him he could go get it if he wanted it. He won't bother anything."

I nodded slowly. "Okay, well, I'll let Dan know he can go inside then—"

"I wouldn't," Joe warned. "Dad's never met him, and you know how his memory is. He's as bad as Mom sometimes. If he thinks Dan's trying to break in or something... I just wouldn't want either of them to get hurt. Here, let me call Dad and see what's going on. Once he's gone, Dan can put the soup in the fridge. It shouldn't take but just a few minutes. He's probably already gone." He glanced around the room then picked up his phone from the nightstand. "I'll go out in the hall to call so you can call Dan and tell him what's going on."

"You don't have to go out in the hall—"

"It's fine," he said lightly, waving off my concern. As he moved past me and out the door, he looked back to say, "Tell him sorry it worried him."

The dry comment had nothing genuine in it, but he was gone before I could respond anyway.

I stood in silence, trying to listen to whatever conversation was going on outside the door, though I could only hear the murmur of his voice echoing in the hallway. I moved forward, checking the peephole, but as soon as I did, the handle twitched, and he was back inside. A lump formed in my throat at the wide-eyed expression he wore.

"Well?"

"Uh... Dad said he'd been gone for a while," he said, the blood all drained from his cheeks. "Is Dan still there? Can you call him?"

"Yeah, why?"

"Have him check and see if someone's there—"

"I'm not putting him in danger!"

"Just have him walk past and see if he can hear anything. Maybe Dad didn't get the door latched all the way. With the storm blowing like it is, it probably just pushed the door open. We just need him to check so we don't waste the police's time."

About that, I could agree, especially since I had no desire for him to actually want me to call the police and find out this had all been a ruse. I held up my phone, pretending to type a message. "I'll text him—"

"Just call—" he argued, trying to get around to see what I was doing. "This is serious!"

I pressed my back against the wall. "Shhh! He's already texting me back." I shook my head, staring at my screen. Joe's panic was starting to scare me. This had been a bad idea. I was going to be found out. To my relief, he stopped trying to get a look at my screen, checking his own phone instead. "He's going to check now. He said he didn't hear anything, so maybe you're right. Maybe it was just the storm," I told him, reading the fake message aloud. He seemed to breathe easier as I did. "Hey, how did he get inside anyway?"

He glanced at his phone. "I told him about the key above the door." He paused, looking back up at me.

"He won't use it any other time, and I told him to make sure he puts it back."

"Oh." I had no idea my husband even knew about the key. I stared at my phone for a few seconds more, then held it up, my voice breathless. I no longer cared if I sounded convincing. "He says there's no one there. Just the storm, I guess."

"Phew," Joe said, a hand on his chest as he let out a sigh of relief. "Good." He walked past me, flopping down on the bed. "Crisis averted."

"Crisis averted," I repeated weakly, a quivering smile on my lips as I thought about the key I'd believed to be my secret. I wondered what else my husband might know about.

And how I'd managed to know so little.

CHAPTER SEVENTEEN

When we awoke the next morning, the storm had subsided, and the roads were mostly cleared, but everything was still bathed in thick blankets of snow. I stared out the hotel window into the bright-white parking lot, my breath making clouds of condensation on the pane.

His hands slipped around me from behind, under my shirt, his cool fingers cupping my waist. I shivered.

"Looks like we got a lot more than they expected, hm?" he asked, his stubble scratching my cheek.

"Looks like it."

His voice was a low growl in my ear. "It's so cold out. I wish we could just hole up here and never leave this room. Never leave the bed." He slowly trailed his hands upward.

"You do, do you?" Did I sound as lifeless to him as I did to myself? As if I were reading cue cards.

Apparently not, as he turned me around, pressing his lips to mine gently. He held my face, tucking my hair behind both ears. "I do." His eyes burned with passion as he said the words he'd said to me at the altar not so long ago. Then, it was the happiest moment of my entire life. Now, I felt nothing.

"I'm still feeling a little off." I rubbed my stomach rhythmically.

"Oh." Disappointment weighed on his face, the wrinkles next to his eyes deepening. "But you never got sick last night." His hand went to my forehead. "And you aren't running a fever."

"I know. I'm sorry, I just don't want to give you something if I've caught a bug."

"It's worth the risk to me." He pressed his body to mine, his hands gripping my biceps as he willed me to meet his eye.

I couldn't keep coming up with excuses to avoid him, though truth be told, I *did* feel queasy—just not because I was sick. Either way, I closed my eyes as he lowered his head slowly, pressing our mouths together once more.

My breathing quickened, and I struggled to catch my breath, but he didn't seem to notice. Instead, his hand slipped under my shirt, running his fingers under the edge of my bra. My body was cold as he moved us toward the bed, pulling my shirt over my head quickly.

In an instant, my bra was off, and he'd lowered his mouth to my breasts, the heat of his breath in the cool room feeling undeniably good. He pulled back, easing me down onto the bed.

I squeezed my eyes shut, turning my head as I felt the first tear fall. I could do this.

I wouldn't think about her.

Not here.

He was *my* husband.

He'd married me. Had chosen me.

Maybe he was right.

Maybe the photos didn't belong to him, however unlikely.

I forced myself to believe it, if only for the moment. It was the only way I'd be able to stomach what came next.

As he slowly removed my pants and then his own, my stomach filled with betraying desire. I didn't *want* to want him. I didn't want to fall into old patterns. I didn't want it to feel as good as it did.

Or...maybe I did. I couldn't decide.

New tears filled my eyes, and suddenly, he was inside of me, either not seeing the tears or ignoring them altogether.

"I love you," he whispered, moving rhythmically between my legs. We were in two separate worlds—his filled with pleasure and mine filled with heartache, neither of us able to cross the void that separated us.

"I love you, Edie," he repeated more forcefully.

I couldn't bring myself to say it back. I couldn't bring myself to say anything. If I opened my mouth, I feared I'd only be able to release the sobs I was fighting desperately to keep inside. My body was acting against my heart and mind, reacting to him in a way that had him groaning with pleasure, but still, the tears trailed down my cheeks, and I couldn't quite breathe.

When he backed away from me suddenly, practically throwing himself backward, I let out a ragged gasp as if I could catch my breath for the first time.

"*Are you crying?*" His voice cracked with genuine concern.

I shook my head, but we both knew it was a lie.

He reached for my face, but I covered my eyes with my hands, drying my cheeks angrily. I *was* angry—with him and with myself.

"What's wrong? You're... You're shaking. You're crying." His hand rested on my wrist, gently willing it away so he could look at me. "Did I hurt you? Did something happen?"

If I tried to speak, I was sure I'd either vomit or burst into sobs. Instead, I said nothing. I shook my head, shivering. I was too cold but unable to move. His fingers twirled in my hair, a thumb dusting across my cheek.

"Are you really feeling that badly?"

I nodded, my bottom lip quivering from the cold.

He checked my forehead again. "I'm so sorry, Edie, I... I thought you were just trying to punish me by being difficult." He gave a breathless laugh, then brushed another tear from my cheek. "If I'd known you truly didn't feel good, I... I mean, you know I'd never... You should've stopped me." He ran a hand over his face, mumbling to himself, then scrambled to gather his clothes. "What is it that's hurting? Your stomach still? You're still shaking..."

Was I?

"You look like you're going to be sick." He felt my cheeks again, then my head. "Maybe I should try to get out and get some medicine. You do feel a little warm."

Was he lying? Or was I really sick?

At that moment, I couldn't have said.

He reached for his coat—the red of the material flashing in front of my eyes—then his scarf and hat. "I'll run down and see if they have anything in the lobby. If not, I'll check the store across the street. Will you be okay while I'm gone?"

I nodded—at least, I think I did.

He touched my back before departing, and when he reached the door, he stopped, hesitating for just a second to say, "I'm sorry, Edith."

I blinked.

"We have to move on, you know?"

Was that what he called this?

What he'd been trying to do? Moving on?

His words said it all. That's what he expected me to do.

"I'll be back soon."

When I didn't respond, he pulled open the door, disappearing into the hall without another word.

Realizing he was gone seemed to have broken whatever spell I was under. Suddenly, I could move again. And *move,* I did. Had to.

I shoved myself up off the bed and rushed toward the restroom, barely making it in time to empty the remnants of last night's tomato soup from my stomach. Something was churning in me, something more than the sickness—if that was even real and not a result of my inner turmoil.

There was no moving on from this. Not until he paid.

CHAPTER EIGHTEEN

When Joe returned, I'd dressed and was sitting curled up on the bed, wrapped in the thick comforter, unable to quell the shaking.

He placed a plastic sack on the end of the bed, stripping out of his many layers as he studied me. "Are you still feeling bad?"

Like I haven't already told you that.

I nodded. "Did you find medicine?"

He pulled out a bottle of pink liquid. "For your nausea. I got pain medicine, too. I know you usually get a headache when you're sick."

"Thanks." I took both medications and the bottle of water he handed me.

"I'm sorry," he said all in one breath as if he'd been waiting to say it. "I truly didn't realize you really didn't feel well. I thought you were just avoiding me."

"Is that what you meant when you left? That we just needed to 'move on'? That's what you were trying to do?"

He pressed his lips together. "I'm not sure what I'm supposed to do, Edith. You can hardly look at me. You won't say you love me. You flinch whenever I touch you." He held out his hand as if he were cupping my cheek, but our skin didn't meet. "I don't know how to handle this. And I just thought, I mean, I thought if I could...remind you of who we used to be. If I could make you remember us—the us that I fought so hard for—maybe you'd come back to me. I knew you weren't into it, but I thought I was helping you come out of whatever *this* is." He gestured toward me.

"What? You thought you'd save me with your magical dick?" I spat.

It was his turn to flinch then, and the hurt in his eyes was palpable. He looked as though he was going to say something, then thought better of it and closed his mouth. He stepped away from me, turning, then spun back again. "You know, I understand that you're hurt, and you're dealing with things in your own way, but did you ever stop to think...if I'm telling you the truth —*which I am*—and if I've done everything you've asked —*which I have*—then maybe, just maybe, you're not being fair to me. I went out in a storm and got your medicine, I took you out to get dinner last night, I brought you here to get away and enjoy ourselves even though we can't afford it, I deleted all my social media and gave you my phone..." He sighed with exasperation. "I've done all I can, Edith. Maybe at some point, you'll realize that. I just hope you haven't completely pushed me away when we reach that point."

My jaw was decidedly less stiff as I watched him packing our clothes into our bags. "What are you doing?"

He didn't bother glancing up. "Check out's in an hour. I'll pack everything and get it loaded into the car. Just lie there and rest." His tone was bitter. "I'll handle everything."

He packed in silence while I contemplated.

Was he right?

I didn't want to consider it, but he'd put the question in my head.

He was doing so much for me, but I couldn't see past the hurt from before. The pictures and the app now. If he truly didn't put them on his phone, I was being ridiculous. Worse than ridiculous, I was being cruel.

But how could I know the truth?

My husband was an incredible liar, but last time, when I confronted him with enough proof, he'd come clean. Why wasn't he this time? Because he knew the consequences? Or because he wasn't lying anymore?

The only way to find out was to search through his things. To dig deeper. To turn over every stone.

Luckily for me, as he zipped his suitcase and placed it on the floor next to mine, I realized we were going to the very place I'd be able to do that. Our home had all the answers.

I'd never been more ready to go home.

CHAPTER NINETEEN

I spent most of our drive home sleeping, and when I wasn't asleep, I pretended to be. I couldn't face him right then—so torn by disgust, anger, and worry. There was a deep pit of stress gnawing at me, wondering now if I had it wrong all along.

I didn't want to believe it, but I couldn't deny that what he'd said had worked. It had caused me to doubt myself. Even more so than before.

To doubt what I believed. How would I ever come back from the way I'd treated him if I was wrong about everything?

He lugged the bags inside the apartment, inspecting both the handle and the lock on our door. I followed closely behind him, rubbing sleep from my eyes as he looked around, searching to make sure nothing was out of place. Once he was satisfied, he carried the bags to our bedroom while I moved to the kitchen, my stomach rumbling for something to eat for the first time all day.

Thinking quickly, I poured a can of soup into a bowl, searching the fridge for a bag of takeout I could throw away, in case Joe searched for evidence that Dan had been here. Once I'd taken care of that, I pulled down the loaf of bread, preparing two peanut butter sandwiches.

The soup was still cooling in the bowl, and two peanut butter sandwiches lay in front of me when Joe reappeared. He took in the scene, his gaze trailing over the small table in the center of our eat-in kitchen. I lifted a spoonful of broth to my lips, blowing on it gently before slurping it down.

"It doesn't look like anything was touched," he told me, running a hand across his jaw.

"That's good."

"Yeah, I just double-checked everything to be sure. Looks like you're feeling better. Is that the soup Dan brought you?" He pointed to the fridge, still staring at the food without moving toward me. I knew he was waiting for an invitation, and I extended it cautiously by pushing one of the sandwiches toward him.

"Here you go," I said.

Looking relieved, he sank down in the chair across from me, eyeing the sandwich.

"It's not poisoned..." I said with a playful eye roll.

His laugh eased the tension. "Are you sure?" He picked up the sandwich and took two ravenous bites.

"Thank you. I was starving," he admitted once he'd swallowed them, brushing a glob of peanut butter from the corner of his mouth with a sheepish grin.

"Look, Joe, I should..." I placed my spoon down, smoothing my hands in front of me. "I should apologize to you. I mean, I've been awful lately."

His eyes widened with obvious shock, but he didn't argue or say anything. Instead, he placed his food down, too, giving me his full attention as he dusted the crumbs from his hands and waited for me to go on.

"I don't know what's going on with the pictures, but they scared me. Before, when you...well, I mean, when I found out that you'd cheated on me, that was the worst day of my life. I can't..." I touched my throat. "I still can't quite breathe when I think about it. It's the worst feeling..." I trailed off, spying the frustration in his eyes. That wasn't the point of this conversation. We'd already dealt with that. "Anyway, when I saw the pictures, it was like I was living that moment all over again. I mean, *I was* living that moment all over again. The floor swept out from under me, and my chest was tight, and I just thought, *please, not again. Please.*" I felt tears stinging my eyes, and he reached across the table, taking my hand.

"Look, you don't have to—"

"No, please just let me finish," I cut him off with an apologetic smile. "I made a lot of mistakes that day because I was so scared. I didn't want to listen to what you had to say. I had my mind made up. And that wasn't fair to you. Because... I do love you, Joe." He exhaled as if he'd been holding his breath for days waiting to hear me say so. "I love you so much. And the idea of losing you was enough to kill me."

His hand slipped under mine, so he was holding it with both hands. "You were never going to lose me, Edith. I swore to you I was going to be better. And I meant it. I'd never forgive myself if I hurt you again. I don't know how the pictures got there either, and maybe I didn't handle it the best. We're both to blame. I was embarrassed and confused and...angry—with you, for not trusting me, and with me, for ever giving you a reason not to. I will do whatever it takes to prove to you they weren't mine and that I've never cheated on you again. Just name it."

It was my turn to pat his hand, and I did so with my head tilted toward my shoulder in sympathy. "Can we just move on? Move past it and forget it happened?"

"I'd love that." He beamed, lifting my hands to his lips and pressing them to my fingers. "I love you."

"I love you." This time, I knew it wasn't a lie. I could say it without bile rising in my throat.

"So, we're good?" he asked.

"We're good." I dusted a tear from the corner of my eye.

Releasing my hands finally, he took another bite of his sandwich. "So, what do you want to do with the rest of our day?"

"Well, we'll have to go back to work tomorrow, I'm sure, so I was thinking it would be nice to have a lazy day here, especially with the snow still on the ground. We could watch movies and drink cocoa."

Shoving the last bite of his sandwich into his mouth, he dusted his hands on his pants and stood. "Couldn't have planned it better myself."

He prepared the cocoa while I went to the living room, eating the last of my soup and sandwich on the couch as I scrolled through our streaming accounts in search of a feel-good movie or sitcom. I'd been lucky in that Joe and I preferred the same sort of shows. Occasionally, I'd be in the mood for a thriller or romance, or he'd be interested in the latest action movie, but for the most part, either of us was perfectly happy watching *The Office*, *Friends*, or *Brooklyn Nine-Nine* year-round. It was one of the first things we'd bonded over, actually, our love of goofy sitcoms. I wished I could go back to those days and see my husband through the eyes I once had.

We'd never had the money to afford therapy after his affair, but what I'd looked up online said it could be hard to ever see them in a different light once they'd shown themselves that way. Was that what was happening? Was I going to be suspicious of him for the rest of my life? Would I always assume the worst of him?

I was still struggling to decide how I was feeling, as I had been for days, when Joe appeared and set our mugs of cocoa on the coffee table. He sat down next to me, his arm around my shoulder as I turned on a rerun of *Superstore* and rested my head on his chest, inhaling his minty cologne. I felt safe here with him.

Something had changed.

Everything had changed.

I didn't realize it just yet, but then again, I did. I felt something shifting inside me, bringing me back to him, wanting to accept the excuse he'd given me. It was all that mattered. He loved me. I loved him.

We could move on.

It was the only option.

At least, that's what I told myself.

CHAPTER TWENTY

My shift didn't start until noon the next day, giving me the perfect window to go through our accounts while Joe was at work. I kissed him at the door, still pretending everything was fine and at least partially conflicted over whether or not I was actually pretending.

I was confusing myself at that point...changing my mind from one moment to the next. I flashed back to all the warnings in health class growing up—*this is your brain on drugs*—and had to imagine my decision-making skills, emotions, and ability to focus were nearly as impaired.

This is your brain on heartbreak, kids.

As I shut the door, I moved back into the house and toward the window in our kitchen, where I could see the parking lot and watch for him to leave. I stood back from the window, peering through the open blinds, though not close enough that he might see me if he were to look over as I watched the black sedan back out of his parking spot and then out of the lot altogether.

Once it had, I puffed out a breath of air and closed the curtains, dimming the light in the room. My body trembled with anticipation and fear of being caught. He had no reason to return home, but that didn't stop the worry billowing inside me.

In the bedroom, I eased down in front of the desk, tugging at the drawers.

As Dan had said, they were locked. The key would've been small and silver if it matched the keyholes, but I'd never seen anything of the sort lying about. In fact, Joe had never once mentioned that he kept these drawers locked in the first place.

How could I ask him without alerting him to the fact that I was suspicious of him? And, if he knew that, I was sure whatever evidence might be in these drawers wouldn't be there any longer.

No, I'd have to find another way. Only one drawer —the top right—was unlocked. When I pulled it open, an array of pens, pencils, and sticky notes scattered noisily. I moved my hand through the drawer, pressing my hands on the back of it just in case, but found nothing that might help. Slamming it shut, I crawled under the desk, looking up to see if he'd taped the key there for safekeeping. Still, there was nothing. Every trick I'd ever seen in a movie or read in a book was proving useless.

Next, I walked to my bedside table and pulled out a bobby pin, bringing it back and using the end to attempt to pick the lock. As I expected, that did little other than bend my hairpin to an unusable shape and frustrate me further.

I stood, exasperated, and stared around the room, clicking my tongue.

I wasn't going to allow myself to be helpless or to give up. I needed to find wherever he kept the key. I had to open this drawer, no matter what.

Truth be told, I wasn't sure if I was hoping to find a juicy secret inside the depths of the drawers at all. On the one hand, I'd much rather find out my husband hadn't been lying, and the drawers were only locked to conceal our passwords and account numbers. On the other hand, this was quite a lot of work for nothing to come of it.

The next place I checked was his nightstand. I dug through the drawers, running my hands along the bottom of his socks and underwear in search of something—anything, really—but to no avail.

I lifted the lamp. Checked under the mattress and under the bed. I looked through the closet, sifting things this way and that. Searched the pockets of his pants and opened the suitcase he'd just unpacked. The one he'd be packing to go to his parents' house tomorrow.

When I moved it, I heard a rattling sound that caused me to freeze.

I shook the suitcase carefully, listening.

Yes, there was definitely something there.

I laid it flat, running my hands across the interior fabric slowly, trying to locate the source of the sound. Near the top right corner, I made contact with something solid. Something just beneath the thin fabric. I traced the outline of something with my fingertips, my throat dry as I felt sure that I'd found a key. This had to be *the* key I was looking for. Why on earth was it hidden in his suitcase?

I unzipped the liner carefully, revealing the metal bars that connected to the handle, and shook the bag, expecting the key to fall loose. When it didn't, I stuck my hand inside the lining and felt near the top.

There.

The key had been taped to the top corner, though one side had come loose, allowing it to rattle against the metal bars when I shook the suitcase. I tore it free easily, pulling it out and resting it in my palm. I stared down at the small silver key. One much like I'd imagined. Could this really be it?

Pushing the suitcase aside, along with my apprehension, I moved out of the closet and back to the desk. Without allowing myself to second-guess anything, I pushed the key into the drawer closest to me and turned it with a flick of my wrist.

Click.

I was in.

I tugged the drawer open and stared down at the

manila envelopes that held various things. I'd seen inside the drawer before, and this was what it had always held. Our lease, health insurance information, bills we were still paying off. The familiar green notebook was at the front of the drawer, and I pulled it out too, flipping through it.

Just like I'd remembered, there was a page filled with our various accounts and all of the passwords. I stood from the floor, sitting in the chair in front of the desk and searching for the website of our bank.

I typed in his username, copied and double-checked the password, and clicked **Sign in.** A red box popped up instantly, letting me know I had the wrong username or password. My breathing caught, my hands suddenly cold. Had he changed the password without updating the sheet?

Dan was right, wasn't he?

He was hiding something.

I couldn't risk putting in the info wrong again—I wasn't sure how many attempts I had until he was locked out. Instead, I used the key to open the drawer above the already open one.

There, I found nothing of note. A few bills, an old dental X-ray, and a photograph of him and his class during a field trip. I ran a finger over the dusty photo, studying his face.

Who are you, Joe?

Who are you really?

The sudden sound of my phone vibrating caused

me to jolt. I shut the drawer quickly, lifting my phone from the desk and staring at his name.

"Hello?"

Joe let out a heavy sigh. "Hey, were you trying to log into my bank account?"

My blood ran cold, my head swimming with fear and possibilities. Should I lie? Should I be honest? Truth was, I had no idea what I was going to do until the words came out of my mouth.

"Um, no... Why?"

"I got an email from the bank saying someone had attempted to log in. It wasn't me, so I was hoping it was you."

"Oh no. They didn't get in, did they? Do you think it could be related to the break-in? Maybe someone got in between the time your dad left and Dan arrived?" Or maybe someone came back after Dan left. It was the only real possibility, but I had to keep my reality and the reality I was spinning for Joe separate. *No.* No one had tried to hack the account. Right. It was me.

I was losing my sense of reality altogether, it seemed.

How could anyone manage to keep so many lies straight?

"I'm not sure. I only got one email... I'm not sure if they get multiple chances before they get locked out. Either way, I'd feel better knowing my password has been changed. Could you do me a favor and reset it?"

"Um... I—"

"Or have you already left for work?" He cursed under his breath. "If you have, I'll reset it once I get to the school."

"No, no, it's fine. I'm still here. Let me get over to the computer." I made noise, shuffling things around on the desk in an attempt to make it sound as if I was making my way across the room and sitting down. "Is your password in the green notebook?"

"Yep."

I paused. "The drawers are locked."

"Oh, right. Sorry, I keep the key hidden in my suitcase. If you unzip the inside, it's in the upper lefthand corner."

"Since when do you lock it at all?" I asked, pacing the room with the key already in my hand.

"I always have. It has all of our passwords and everything. You didn't think I'd leave that unlocked, did you?" He gave a half laugh.

"No, I guess not. Ahh... Okay, I've got the key." I moved back toward the desk and fumbled with the drawers. "Here's the notebook."

"Good, it should be on the first page."

I opened the notebook, reading over the username and password combination I'd already tried once, and typed it slowly. Before I pressed enter, I read it aloud to him. "Is that right?"

"Yep, that's it."

I pressed enter, waiting for the red button to appear, and froze, my breathing catching.

"Did it work?"

"Um..." I stared at the screen, surprised to find myself looking at his account after all. "Y-yeah. I'm in."

"Okay, good. Can you just change it to something else and update the book? Our anniversary instead of my birthday, maybe?"

"Mhm..." It was all I could bring myself to say. How had it worked this time?

"Thanks, babe. Love you. Talk to you later, okay?"

I'm not sure whether I said it back or if I responded at all. The next thing I knew, the call had ended, and I was trying to piece together what had just happened. I scrolled through his transactions, searching for...what? I didn't know.

Moments earlier, I'd been sure his account would hold some sort of damning evidence, but as far as I could tell, there was nothing.

His direct deposit went into his account once a month, like usual. Money came out for bills, gas, occasional fast food, the hotel last night... Groceries came out of my checks, but there were a few odds and ends purchases at the grocery store. Nothing that added up to anything. All in all, there was nothing suspicious.

But then, he'd known that, hadn't he? Otherwise, why would he have let me access the account? If there was something to hide, why would he have let me change his password?

And why did the incorrect password suddenly work? Could he have gotten a notification about me trying to access his account and then changed it back to what the book said, maybe?

But why? It wasn't as if he could change his transaction history. He couldn't go through and delete or rename transactions to cover his tracks. What I was looking at now was what I would've been looking at if I'd gotten access the first time. So why had he changed his password to keep me out?

Maybe he didn't.

Maybe I'd typed it wrong the first time.

But I'd been so careful...

I scrolled back further, desperately hoping to find something, anything, that would make me feel like this witch hunt was validated. With each passing month, I felt less and less sure, the small bit of hope in my stomach dissipating.

There was nothing. Nothing he was trying to hide.

Groaning with frustration, I exited out of the browser, updated the notebook, and placed it back in the drawer. As I went to shut the top drawer, I froze. There was a picture frame in the far back corner of the drawer. A small five-by-seven turned upside down. It was wedged in the back, between notebooks and other odds and ends and, if I wasn't sitting at this exact angle from having leaned down to the drawer below it, I might not have seen it.

I reached in with a cautious hand, as if the frame might bite, and took hold of it, pulling it to safety. When I turned it over in my hand, something within my lower stomach tensed. The photo was of my husband with another woman.

A woman I didn't recognize.

Not Amma.

Not me.

None of his coworkers.

His arm was draped over her shoulder, and they were both clad in winter gear—ear warmers and thick coats. They smiled down at the camera, looking bright and full of hope.

The cheerfulness in their expressions was a stark contradiction to the shattered glass they hid behind.

Why was the glass broken?

Why was the picture hidden?

Why did he have it?

Most importantly, who was this woman?

CHAPTER TWENTY-ONE

When I returned to work that afternoon, the picture frame was safely back in its hiding place while I worked out what I should do with it. On the one hand, I wanted to ask him about it. Perhaps there would be a reasonable explanation. On the other hand, there was a good chance he'd just lie to me. For now, I had the advantage. I just had to figure out how to use it.

"Table eight needs refills," Amma said as she skittered past me, obviously irritated.

"On it," I said, trying to recall what I'd brought them to drink in the first place. She beat me to the drink station, refilling six glasses at once with a precision that only came from someone who'd been at this a long time.

I waited patiently, smiling at her when she glanced at me, though the gesture wasn't returned.

"Is...everything okay?" I asked. Amma had never been overly friendly to me, but since my return that day, her attitude had grown colder. It was as if I'd done something to offend her.

She pressed her lips together, pulling the drinks back one by one and placing them on the tray on the counter. "Mhm. Fine." She moved past me without another word.

Moments later, I placed a set of refills down in front of my guests. "Here you go. Sorry about that wait. Is there anything else I can bring you right now?"

"No, we're alright," said the man as his wife struggled to wipe a bit of food from the squirming toddler's mouth.

"Okay, well, just let me know if you need anything else."

I turned away, checking on my two other tables and promising to return with a piece of pie for the gentleman at table six.

All the while, I kept an eye on Amma.

To my surprise, she seemed to be keeping an eye on me, too. Twice, when I looked up to search for her, I'd found her watching me.

After bringing the pie to my table and closing out another, I brought the plates back to the kitchen and saw her step into the break room. As the last of my tables were clearing out, I delivered their checks and checked the time.

It was still early in my shift for lunch, but it was

also a slow point just after the lunch rush, so I took a chance in asking Jenna if I could go to lunch a bit early.

"Are your tables empty?"

"Yep, just cleared them."

She glanced at the clock from where she stood in the storage room, doing inventory. "Okay, then. Ask Alexis to cover your section. Is everything okay?"

"Fine." I patted my stomach with a grin. "I just didn't get a chance to eat breakfast this morning."

She nodded slowly. "Have some real food then. None of that cardboard stuff." She glanced over my shoulder. "Ask Manny to fix you whatever you'd like."

"Oh, no, it's okay... Honestly, I'm—"

"I insist. It's on me. I need you to be full and alert."

"Okay, thanks." I felt awkward—like the charity case I desperately didn't want to be—but, as I stepped away from her and back to the kitchen, my stomach began growling in anticipation. The food served at Jenna's always smelled delicious, and I felt certain it would taste even better.

I ordered soup, something simple that was already hot, and carried my bowl into the break room. When Amma noticed me—glancing up from her phone with a hardened expression—she didn't say a word.

"Hey... Sorry, I don't mean to interrupt."

"I'm almost done," she said, her gaze falling back to her phone. I sat down across from her, the room utterly silent except for the hum of the refrigerator. I needed to find a way to talk to her since that was the whole reason for me being there, but she wasn't making it easy.

What did Joe see in this woman? Sure, she was beautiful and bright and fun when she needed to be, but couldn't he see through the facade she put on? This was the real Amma. This gruff, quiet, angry version I kept meeting firsthand. I'd seen her laughing and having fun with the other workers, but when it was just the two of us, she was different. Was I the only one she treated like this? Was it because Jenna wasn't around? Because I was the new girl? Because I had nothing to offer her?

Or maybe...

My breathing hitched as I considered the possibility.

Maybe she knows who I am.

No.

I had to believe she didn't. If she did, surely Joe would've found out that I'd switched jobs by now. If she did, surely he'd have said something to me.

"That looks good," I said, pointing to the wrap she was eating.

She took a bite, nodding.

I swirled my spoon through my soup thoughtfully, trying to decide what else to say.

"Hey, Amma?"

She looked up at me, the wrinkle in her forehead deepening. She had just the one wrinkle, a single, deep line that ran across her forehead when she raised her brows. Somehow, it made her even more endearing. Not even wrinkles could affect her beauty.

"Yeah?"

I stirred faster, needing to busy my hands. "Um, I just wondered, I mean... Are we... Are we okay?"

"Why wouldn't we be?" came the quick response.

It wasn't a yes.

"I just thought... Never mind." I shook my head, looking down. I lifted the spoon to my lips, blowing on it gently.

She stood, dropping the final bit of her lunch in the trash and washing her hands. When she turned around, she paused, staring at me as if she were going to say something, then thought better of it. With two more steps toward the door, she stopped again. This time, when she looked at me, her expression was rife with indignation. "I don't like it when people take advantage of Jenna."

Whatever I'd been expecting her to say, that wasn't it. I processed what she'd said slowly, trying to make sense of it. "I-um, sorry, what? You think I'm taking advantage of her?"

She crossed her arms over her chest. "I know you are. You haven't been here six months and already took two days off without putting in a vacation request like the rest of us have to. Somehow you've convinced her you can only work the day shift. You know, there are rules around here... A hierarchy. Those of us who've been here and put in our time, even we don't get away with stuff like that—not because we can't, but because we respect her too much to do that to her. Do you know who worked the shifts you missed?"

"Amma, I'm so sorry. It's not what you think, I'd never—"

"Because I'll tell you. It was Jenna. She didn't ask us to pick up the slack because she never does. She does it herself without complaint. Jenna's kind, and people take advantage of that. But, even if she won't say it, I will. That's not how things work around here. Anywhere else, and you'd have been fired for calling in two days in a row when you're so new. But instead, you just come back here like it's normal..." She paused to catch her breath, her neck flushing pink.

"I'm really sorry. I promise I'm not trying to take advantage of Jenna. You're right, she is nice. She's been very kind to me, and I'm sorry if you think that I'm not treating her fairly. This week was a fluke. It won't happen again. I've told her that. I can't afford to miss that much work anyway. It was just..." I couldn't possibly explain it. "It won't happen again."

"Why are you here, Edith?" she asked, something dark in her tone.

"B-because I needed a job."

"Do you? Because those of us who do need jobs, we don't cut out in the middle of the week without notice, we don't forget to check on our tables and get lousy tips..."

"I'm just getting the hang of things. I've never worked in a restaurant before—"

"That's no excuse. You're here now." She pointed her finger down firmly. "I'm just letting you know... We're watching you. All of us. And if we think you're taking advantage of her, we're going to make sure she gets rid of you. One way or another."

"I understand..." I said softly, not meeting her eyes. "I promise you that's not what I'm trying to do."

She shrugged one shoulder, moving toward the coat rack and unzipping the mustard-yellow handbag. She pulled out a white bottle of vitamins and a lozenge, dropping a vitamin into her hand.

I saw the wording on the vitamin bottle at the same time the scent of the lozenge hit me.

Ginger. For nausea.

"Prenatal vitamins?" I asked, my voice barely above a whisper.

She tucked them back in her purse, zipping it up carefully. "Yeah, so?"

"I..." My vision blurred, the room suddenly spinning too fast and too slow all at once. Maybe it was getting smaller? "I didn't know."

"Why would you?" She picked up her bottle of green tea from the table and downed the pill.

"C-congratulations," I muttered. At least, I think I did. Maybe I didn't say anything at all.

"You okay?"

I sank down in the chair. No, I'd already been

sitting. Hadn't I? Nothing made sense. Bile rose in my throat as I realized she was still staring at me, waiting for a response. "I-I'm fine." I placed a hand to my chest. "Sorry, just...got a bit light headed. It's my blood sugar."

She stared at me for a moment longer, a single brow raised. Then, apparently accepting that as explanation enough, she pulled open the door, allowing the sound from the noisy dining room into the once-silent space.

"See you out there."

I nodded, placing my head in my hands once she'd left.

Pregnant? How was it possible she was pregnant?

Was it Joe's? Or Phillip's?

This changed everything.

CHAPTER TWENTY-TWO

When I got home from work that evening, the thick scent of burgers hit me before I'd made it inside. Opening the door pulled a thick cloud of smoke toward me. I peered through the hazy apartment, making my way through the living room and into the kitchen.

"You're going to have to open a window," I told him, pulling open the one above our sink. "It's a wonder the smoke alarm didn't go off."

"Oh, it doesn't work," he said simply, turning to face me and popping a fry into my mouth.

"It doesn't?"

"No, er, well, I guess it does. It *would*, anyway, if it had batteries in it."

I looked up at the white, circular alarm overhead, noticing the empty space where a battery should've gone. "What happened?"

"Remember? It was beeping a few weeks ago."

"Yeah, I remember. I thought you replaced the batteries, not that you'd taken them out altogether."

"Well, I meant to, but I'd forgotten. Good thing now, hm?"

"Not really."

"I'll pick them up when I'm out this weekend and get them replaced. Promise."

"You're going to leave me in an apartment without a working smoke detector? All alone?"

"You've already been here for weeks without one. What's a few more days?" He ate another fry, leaning across me to pull down two plates from the cabinet.

"Forget it. I'll get them myself."

He placed the plates down, resting against the counter with both hands on his hips. "Bad day?"

"No," I lied.

He held his hand out, wiggling his fingers in preparation to tickle me. "I don't believe you," he sang.

I shied away from him, bracing myself for what was coming just as he turned his attention back to our dinner. He flipped off the burner and placed the burgers on slices of bread, dividing the fries out onto our plates.

"I need to ask you about something."

The smoke had all but cleared as he turned to face me again. "Okay, shoot."

"Today, when I was going through the desk

drawers in the bedroom, when I had to reset your password—"

"Mhm." He nodded.

"I found a picture frame with you and another woman."

He stared at me for a moment, his face unchanging. "Another woman?"

"Yes. She was brunette. Twenties. You were younger, too. She might've been an ex, maybe? You guys were wearing coats, dressed for winter. The frame was broken. I'd never seen her before, never seen that picture before."

He scratched his jaw. "I'm not sure who you could be talking about. Maybe a cousin or something."

"Why would you have it in the drawer?"

"I didn't realize I did," he said. "I brought the desk from my parents' house, so maybe it was one of their pictures."

"Can I show you?" I asked, already making my way out of the kitchen.

"Is it really important?" He followed close behind me. "I'm starving."

"I just want to know," I told him. "It'll only take a second." In the bedroom, I retrieved the key from its hiding place and unlocked the drawer. He stood on the far side of the room, his back resting against the wall as I pulled it open.

My face burned with anticipation—so desperate for answers, any answers of any kind.

I reached my hand back, feeling for the frame.

"Here it is." My hand connected with it, and I pulled it out, revealing the photo behind the broken glass.

He crossed the room, eyes narrowing. When he was close enough to make it out, he swallowed, taking the frame. "Oh."

"Oh? Who is she?"

"It's..." A hand went to cover his mouth. "It's Lizzie."

My stomach seized with intense recognition.

Lizzie.

His ex-wife.

His dead ex-wife.

"I had no idea I still had this," he said breathlessly, running a finger across the shattered glass. "Where did you say you found it?"

"It was in here." I pointed to the drawer I'd taken it from. "Kind of up in the corner, toward the back. I was on the floor putting the notebook back, and I just happened to see it when I opened that drawer."

"It must've gotten broken in the drawer." He sniffled. "I'm sorry. I... I didn't mean for—"

"No." I knew he was upset, and this went beyond lying. Lizzie was a sensitive subject for him. The first woman he'd ever loved, and she'd died young. A terrible accident. "You don't have to apologize." I put a hand on his shoulder. "Maybe we could get a new frame for it."

"You'd be okay with that?" he asked, still clutching the frame. I wondered how long it had been since he'd seen a picture of her. Or spoken about her at all.

I'd tried to be understanding about it all. As much as I hated to think about Joe being with someone else, being married to someone else, I knew he'd loved Lizzie. And so, if I had to live with a picture of her in our home, it was what I'd have to do. I hated the idea that he'd hidden the picture away for fear of angering me.

"Of course I would."

He pulled me into a hug, kissing the top of my head. "I'd really like that."

"I'm sorry I accused you of..." My voice grew faint. I hadn't truly accused him of anything, but he seemed to understand.

"I get it." He squeezed me a final time before releasing me and making his way toward his night-stand. He placed the photograph down, wiping away a stray tear he was trying to keep me from seeing. "Let's go eat, hm?"

"I'm starving," I agreed, lacing my fingers through his as we walked back toward the kitchen.

And so, I had my answer.

A simple one at that.

Another clue that belonged to a different puzzle altogether.

But each wrong stone only led me closer to turning

over the right one, and so I wouldn't allow myself to lose hope that I'd figure out the truth.

Amma was pregnant. I couldn't forget that. What I needed to do now was find out whose child it was. Find out if Joe knew. Find out what it would mean for us.

Those were the questions I couldn't ask just yet.

But something deep in my bones told me it was nearly time. For now, I just had to keep digging.

CHAPTER TWENTY-THREE

Joe's arms snaked around my waist as I stared into the dark abyss of our bedroom. His gentle snores reminded me that, for some people, all was right in the world. For others, nothing was right. Nothing was right at all.

Since the revelation about Amma, everything had changed for me.

I couldn't stop thinking about it.

Obsessing, maybe.

But it was warranted, wasn't it?

There were two possibilities—one, that she was pregnant by her husband and thrilled, or two, that she was pregnant by mine.

In the beginning, this had all seemed harmless enough. I wanted to know Amma. To understand why my husband had chosen her. With his first affair—the ex—I was never given the courtesy of knowledge. I knew what he'd told me about her—her name and their past—but that was the extent of what I'd found out. He'd insisted that knowing any more would only cause me to spiral and dig deeper into who she was. He'd called me obsessive then, and...well, maybe he had a point. Either way, that time, I'd had no choice but to remain in the dark about it all. This time, I refused to do so.

But getting to know Amma had become a double-edged sword, slicing me deeper with each bit of knowledge I gained.

I needed to find out whose baby she was carrying.

Did Joe know? Was he happy?

Was the baby planned?

No.

It couldn't have been. I believed my husband was capable of many things, but he wasn't evil. If he wanted a baby with another woman, I had to believe he'd leave me first. And what about her husband? The man I'd seen in her doorway, holding her child? Phillip Ashton. Surely he wasn't going to just walk away.

Suddenly, I was filled with a new idea.

I needed to get to her house and meet her husband. I needed to tell him what was going on and...

What?

What good would that do, really?

This affair was tearing my family apart, and as much

as I wanted to see them both pay for that, could I really be the one to tear another family apart out of spite? Could I blow their family up, destroy everything for their baby girl and the innocent husband, if there was another choice?

As much as I wanted to do it, the truth was that it wasn't my place.

Another, lighter thought hit me then: What if this baby was what I'd needed to fix everything? What if, now that Amma was pregnant, she'd break things off with Joe? What if she'd go back to her husband and fix everything?

Maybe he'd never have to know...

If I'd never found those pictures, maybe *I'd* never have known...

The whole thing could end before it began.

No. It had already begun, and I couldn't be delusional enough to think otherwise.

Amma was pregnant and, if they'd ever slept together, there was a chance it was my husband's.

I needed to decide what I was going to do about that.

Sweat gathered at the place where his arm draped over my waist, and ever so slowly, I pulled the blanket up, easing myself away from him and then out of the bed. I stopped, looking back and watching him closely. The blanket rose and fell with his heavy, peaceful breaths.

Oblivious...

But, at least for the moment, I was grateful for his obliviousness.

It meant I had the freedom to do what came next. And what came next would either tear me open or heal my wounds. I just had to be brave enough to go there.

I walked across the room in what felt like slow motion, so completely aware of the sound of his breathing that it became what I set my own breaths to. We were in sync as I lifted his phone from the night-stand softly. Quietly. Praying with everything in me that his deep sleep would continue.

I opened his phone, noticing that his social media icons were back.

This wasn't a shock. His hiatus hadn't lasted long, and he'd told me as much the night before. He was bored without the nearly constant stream of serotonin and dopamine social media provides us with, and I couldn't say I blamed him. I was just as addicted as the next person.

And besides, we were better, weren't we?

That's what he'd had the nerve to ask. And I had to say yes.

I had to.

At that moment, I needed to believe it as much as I needed him to.

But now, I needed to find out what he was hiding. After his affair, I'd started checking his accounts regularly, but eventually, we'd rebuilt the trust, and that had stopped. I felt my heart flutter as I tapped in the passcode and saw the possibilities in front of me.

What to check first?

Any of the three social media apps he frequented?

His messages?

His photos?

What about his call log?

Or apps I didn't recognize at all? My internet research had told me there could be fake apps used to hide dating apps and other things. There were entire worlds, entire websites, entire companies that existed just to help hide secrets and affairs. It was disgusting.

How could anyone profit off another's heartbreak?

I fought down the state of overwhelm and opened his messages first, scrolling through them. There weren't many, thanks to him clearing out his phone during our recent fight. In fact, the only messages there were sent to Sam. I tapped his name, opening the conversation out of pure curiosity. I wondered if there would be anything about the photos.

The last message was from this morning.

Can you cover breakfast? Running late. That was Sam.

Yep. Headed there now.

Yesterday, Joe had asked:

See the email about the meeting after school?

Yep, what do you think it's about?

No idea, was going to ask you to keep me posted.

You won't be there?

Nah, still out. I'll be back tomorrow.

Or not. Maybe they'll tell us at the meeting they're shutting us down.

One can dream.

The day before that, Sam had asked, **Coffee?**

Can't. Won't be in today.

More for me.

That was as far back as the conversation went. Next, I went to his social media, scrolling through those messages, though there weren't many on any of the sites—mostly variations of conversations from him trying to buy or sell something and people offering him a variety of products through their *life-changing, boss-babe* pyramid schemes.

In his call log, the calls that weren't to me, his parents, or the school were from spam numbers in places like Burlington, Vermont, and Fork Union, Virginia. I opened his photos next—the place that had started it all.

To my relief, I didn't immediately see anything to be concerned about.

The photos of Amma were gone—deleted, just like he'd promised.

I scrolled back through a few photos of us and photos of his class. He'd never been one to take a lot of pictures, so there were less than one hundred total like he'd said. It was another reason why the photos of Amma had been so strange. He wasn't the type to take pictures or save them.

I closed out of his photos, a bit of relief filling my gut. The next place to check would be the most difficult—mostly because, if the internet was right, and if it was even there, it would be hiding in plain sight.

I scrolled through his apps. Email, social media, fitness...*yeah, okay*. I couldn't stop my eyes from rolling. I'd never once seen my husband so much as break a sweat from willingly doing physical activity, but when I opened the app, that was indeed what it was for. I tapped a few others, ones I didn't completely recognize, but they ended up being innocent enough. Everything was what it seemed to be.

No lies.

I was preparing to give up and accept that maybe there really was nothing to find. Maybe he'd changed for the better, after all. Maybe I'd finally scared him straight. Then I paused, tilted my head to the side, eyes narrowing, as I stared at the camera app on his phone.

Wait a minute...

I swiped to the next screen.

Aha.

He had two camera apps—nearly identical, were it not for a slight variation in color. One, I recognized as the same one on my own phone. The other, I tapped and was instantly prompted for a passcode.

My jaw tightened, and I glanced over at the bed, suddenly aware it had been too long since I'd checked on him.

I vacillated between using his birthday as usual or trying something different. Surely he wouldn't use his typical passcode on an app he'd taken such care to keep hidden. Going with my gut, I tried our anniversary instead.

The screen buzzed, and a warning flashed above the on-screen keypad.

1 of 3 Attempts

I took another breath. Okay, so maybe he *was* that naive. I tried his birthday. Again, the screen buzzed, the warning growing a brighter, more alarming shade of red.

2 of 3 Attempts

I only had one more chance to get it right, but what in the world could it be? His parents' birthdays, maybe? But I didn't know them, and which would it be anyway? His mom's or his dad's? Perhaps it was the last four of his social security number? I didn't know that offhand, either...

With just one last try, I bit my bottom lip and tapped out my birthday. Everything happened in slow motion, the screen buzzing a final time. The app seemed to self-destruct, the graphics exploding as it promptly returned me to the home screen. My heart thudded in my chest.

The app was gone, his home screen rearranged to replace it as if it had never been there.

But it had. I knew it had.

Whatever it held, he'd obviously put in great effort to hide it. And now, whatever secrets he'd been hiding were gone forever.

CHAPTER TWENTY-FOUR

I hardly slept through the night—worrying about what would happen when Joe noticed the app was gone, wondering what the purpose of the app was in the first place. At one point, I pulled out my phone and searched for answers, but all I could find was the app on the app store. It was a type of "vault" app that destroyed itself if someone tried to gain unauthorized access to it.

It could be used to store pictures, passwords, text and email conversations, other apps, videos, etc.

Essentially, it had likely held all his secrets, and now it was gone.

When his alarm went off, Joe rolled away from me, and I forced my eyes shut, pretending I was still asleep. My stomach churned with worry, the lack of sleep only adding to the sickness I felt. The bed shifted under his weight as he sat up, flipping on the lamp and letting out a loud yawn.

He picked up his phone, and I held my breath, trying to keep it steady despite my erratic heartbeat and sweating palms.

Breathe...

Breathe...

He stood from the bed, and I squeezed my eyes shut even harder, wishing I'd pulled the covers farther around me.

I felt exposed as I lay there.

Waiting...

What would he say when he realized what I'd done? Would he say anything at all? How long would it take him to notice? Would he even notice?

The sound of his bare feet on the floor grew nearer to me.

Breathe...

Breathe...

Breathe...

He opened the bedroom door and shut it behind him. My eyes shot open, a terrified breath escaping my lungs. Maybe I didn't even realize how scared I was until that moment, but as I stared into the darkness, my body trembled with adrenaline and fear. What did I think was going to happen? Did I think he was going to hurt me? My body seemed to hold the secrets my mind did not yet know.

In the morning light, I was realizing what a mistake

I'd made. Why had I let my curiosity get the best of me? I should've been smarter about it. Strategic. I should've confronted him and made him open the app in front of me.

What if it was something for work?

What if it was something important that I'd managed to destroy?

I sat up in bed, suddenly feeling as though I might be sick, and rushed forward, out of the bedroom and into the hall. I hurried into the bathroom, flinging myself onto the ground in front of the toilet with seconds to spare as I felt my dinner fighting its way back up.

My whole body trembled as I attempted to hold my hair back, my knees digging into the cold linoleum floor. Moments later, I heard him walking toward me cautiously, the old floors creaking under his steps.

Not now... Please, not now.

I couldn't find the resolve to care about the app or its contents or Joe's secrets at that moment. All my focus was on ending the sickness.

"Here, let me..."

To my surprise, I felt his hand on my back as he took over, holding my hair.

When it seemed to be over, he stood, flipping on the hot water in the sink. He held his hand under it, waiting for the water to heat up before wetting a wash-cloth and passing it to me. "Are you okay?"

I shook my head, wiping my mouth. I hated what this was doing to me.

Hated it.

"You've been sick a lot lately..." He trailed off, stepping back as I moved to stand. I closed my eyes, thankful the nausea had subsided as I made my way to the sink.

Suddenly, something in his words struck me.

I have *been sick a lot lately, haven't I?*

First at the hotel and now here...

Oh, god...

What if my husband was poisoning me? I eyed him in the reflection over the sink, not wanting to believe it was possible. Then again, what else could—

I froze, a wave of panic spreading through me, its icy grip taking hold of my organs.

No.

No.

No.

I swallowed, shaking my head as I tried to calculate the dates in my mind.

"Joe... I..." I met his eye.

It wasn't possible.

"What's wrong?" He stepped toward me, his head tilted toward his shoulder.

I wiped my mouth again, shaking my head.

No. It was impossible. But I heard myself saying the words anyway.

"I think I'm pregnant."

CHAPTER TWENTY-FIVE

"What do you mean you think you're pregnant?"

I dried my hands, my thoughts spinning as I tried to make sense of it. "I mean, I'm late. Just a few days, but—"

"What? And you're just now noticing?" He ran a hand through his hair, his eyes wide and bulging.

"Well, I mean, I've been a little preoccupied. I just never thought anything of it..."

"But you're on the pill, aren't you? You can't be pregnant." He laughed as if he thought I might join in. As if this were all a big joke. "It's not possible."

I'd started taking the week's worth of placebo pills. When? Two, three days ago? Maybe four? Was I already halfway through? I'd been cramping and tired a lot, so I just assumed my period would start any day. I'd been so busy worrying about Joe that I hadn't stopped to consider any other possibility.

"Well, it's not *im*possible, either. Unlikely, but—"

"And you're sure you took them on time?" he demanded, his face suddenly angry. "You didn't conveniently forget a few?"

My head jerked back, and I was thrown into real time, the room no longer moving in slow motion. "Excuse me? What is that supposed to mean?"

"You've been out of it lately, Edith. We both know that. Maybe you forgot to take a pill or two." He was backtracking, though only slightly. "You've been scattered and all over the place... Would you even notice if you'd forgotten?"

"I haven't forgotten any of my pills." I paused, studying him. Sometimes I felt like I didn't know him at all. "Is that all you meant?"

His eyes danced between mine, obviously trying to decide whether or not to reveal his truest thoughts.

"What exactly are you accusing me of, Joe?"

"I..." He ran a hand over his face, shaking his head. "All I'm saying is that it's convenient timing."

"What is?" Was he going to tell me the truth about Amma? Finally? I held my breath, waiting.

"Well, you've accused me of cheating on you, and now suddenly, you're pregnant."

"Wait, what?" I staggered backward a half step as if I'd been punched. Though I'd heard the insinuation in what he wasn't saying, to hear him come right out with it was humiliating and devastating all at once. "Wait, I'm sorry... Are you accusing me of trying to *trap* you?"

He let out a half breath, as if he was waiting for me to admit it. "I mean, we've been together for three years and never once even had a pregnancy scare. And now, you think you're going to lose me, and suddenly you're pregnant. What am I supposed to think?"

"You're supposed to think that I'm your wife, Joe. And I'd never do that to you. Unlike you, I haven't given you a reason not to trust me." I tried not to think about the app he'd surely find missing sooner or later. Or the lie I'd told about Dan bringing me soup.

"Oh, here we go again." He groaned, turning to look away from me.

"You're the one who brought it up, not me. Yes, I accused you of cheating, but I'm not so desperate that I'd get pregnant just to prevent you from leaving me. Do you honestly think I'm that awful? I love you, but I'm not a monster."

He eased down into a crouching position as if the weight of what he was being told was finally hitting him. "We can't afford a kid right now, Edie."

"I know."

"I... We... I mean, we can't do it. We aren't ready. We'd said maybe in the future, but—"

"I know," I said again, folding my arms across my chest. "First things first, we just need to take a test. It could be a false alarm anyway. We'll take a test, and if it's positive, we'll make an appointment with my doctor. But let's not panic yet."

He nodded, staring into space with outright horror.

Anger swelled in my belly. "And don't worry. I'll let you leave, if that's what you choose. I'll do this on my own." I had no idea if that was true, but I needed to say it after all he'd accused me of. I needed to save some small shred of dignity.

His gaze fell back to me, and he stood, shaking his head with an apologetic stare. "Of course that isn't what I want. I'm sorry. I don't know why I said any of that. I'm just a little bit blindsided by all of this."

"Yeah, well, we all are." He reached for me as I moved past, but I didn't stop. Couldn't.

I moved to our bedroom and shut the door, locking it just as the tears began to fall.

What was I going to do now?

CHAPTER TWENTY-SIX

I was supposed to open with an older waitress named Rose the next morning, so I was shocked when Amma was the one who met me at the door.

"Morning," she said dryly, as if I was the last person she hoped to see there.

"Morning." I moved past her as she held the door open, locking it behind me. "I thought I was scheduled with Rose today?"

"She called in." Offering no further explanation, she turned around, moving back toward the dining room where she was spot mopping what the night shift had missed.

I crossed the restaurant to the break room and slid out of my coat, hanging both it and my purse up on the rack. I washed my hands, as were the rules, then tied my apron around my waist before joining her in the dining room.

I worked behind her, moving chairs back into place once the floors had dried. She was shaking her head, mumbling to herself as she went, though I thought her anger was directed more toward the closing staff than me at that point. The only sounds in the restaurant were coming from the kitchen, where the staff had begun to heat things up and get their supplies ready for the day, but even that was quiet and subdued. Without the constant hum of customers, the restaurant felt like an entirely different place.

"Can I ask you something?" I surprised myself as much as her when I spoke.

She looked up, briefly, with an expression that said she'd rather listen to Ross Geller give a lecture on the Mesozoic era. "Um, sure, I guess. Can't stop you."

"Do you... Do you have any other kids?"

She scrutinized me, and for a moment, I was sure she wasn't going to answer me at all. Finally, she said, "Yeah. I do. A little girl. Why?"

"Oh, I just wondered."

She nodded slowly, then looked back down, continuing her work.

"How old is she?" I busied myself behind her, trying to calm both our nerves by seeming as if I was just making small talk. We were just talking. This was just a conversation.

No need for suspicion here.

"She's two."

"Awww..." I said, practically involuntarily, because that's what you do.

"Why are you asking? And cut the crap about *just wondering*."

"I just wondered," I repeated. "Honestly." I took a deep breath. "It's just...you seem so calm about this pregnancy. I thought you must have experience with it."

She nodded slowly, wiping sweat from her brow before resuming mopping.

"How...how far along are you?" I eyed her stomach, trying to decide if the small bulge I could see was from her apron folds or from the baby now making her its home. My hand went to my own stomach instinctively. After work, I'd stop and buy a test. I needed to know for sure.

"Fourteen weeks," she said. This time, she didn't stop working. "What about you? Do you have kids?"

Apparently no longer suspicious of my intentions—this was the most she'd spoken to me, ever—I supposed this must've been the one thing she was happy to discuss with anyone.

"Um, no. Not...not yet."

She looked back up, triggered by something in my tone, and her eyes fell to where my hand rested on my stomach. "You're pregnant?" I couldn't read her expression. Was it angry? Confused? Frustrated? Shocked?

My hand fell away. One part of me wanted to tell her that yes I was and she should stay away from my husband, thank you very much. The other part said I still didn't know the truth, and I didn't want to start a lie that I'd later have to backtrack if the test came back negative.

"I'm... Well, I think I might be. We'll find out today."

Her brow raised, eyes flicking to my bare finger. I didn't wear my rings at work for fear of ruining them with ketchup or grease stains or losing them in the oversized sink of dirty dishwater. "Who's *we*? Are you married? Boyfriend? *Girl*friend?"

"Husband, yes."

She was quiet for a moment, waiting for me to say more. Finally, she coaxed, "Is he excited?"

"Well..." I meant to tell her it wasn't planned but changed my mind. "Yes, actually, I think he will be." Who cared if Joe told her something else? Should they ever talk about it, I got to spin the narrative first, and I was making it what I wanted it to be. "I'm going to wait to tell him until I know for sure."

She rested her chin against the mop handle.

"I'm...nervous," I admitted, though she hadn't asked. "But excited, too. I guess I've always wanted to be a mom. This might not be the best timing, but..."

"I wouldn't worry about that. It never is."

"No?"

She waved away my concern. "Nah, they say if we

all waited until we were ready to have kids, no one would ever have them."

"Is that true for you? Were you ready when you had your daughter?"

She mulled it over. "I thought I was, I guess. I was married, settled down, we had a house, jobs... But you're never really ready. I had no idea what I was signing up for. None of us ever do."

A commotion in the kitchen interrupted us, followed by a chorus of laughter. Amma rolled her eyes, returning to the sticky spot she'd been mopping up.

"But you're having another one now, so you guys must've made it work...you and your husband," I said quickly, hoping to continue the conversation.

She hesitated, pausing for several seconds, then continued with her work. "Yeah, I mean, I won't say there hasn't been a learning curve, but we've made it work, yes."

"Is he excited about the new baby, then?"

"Mhm."

"I'll bet your little girl is, too."

"Oh, she's thrilled." She paused again, beaming as she said it. Apparently that was the one subject that was entirely allowed. "Although she was disappointed he's not a girl."

My breathing hitched. "You already know what you're having?"

She nodded. "We just found out. My husband's

been vying for a boy, so he was thrilled." She glanced back at me. "What about your husband? Will he want a boy, you think?"

At least she had a husband who wanted a baby. And she was just throwing that all away.

"Yeah, probably." I felt betraying tears pricking my eyes and looked away, but it hadn't gone unnoticed.

Amma stayed where she was, surveying me closely. "They all come around, you know. It all works out."

I sniffled, still unable to look at her. "Oh, yeah, it'll be fine."

"It's scary, in the beginning. Hell, it's always scary. But sometimes men take a little while longer to come around...but they do. Once they hold that baby, they always do."

I met her eyes, wanting to point out how wildly inaccurate that was, but I didn't. Instead, I said, "He'll be a great dad."

"I'm sure he will." Her gaze was sympathetic. Kind. It was the first and only time she'd looked at me that way. "And even if the worst thing happens, the baby will have you. At the end of the day, that's what matters most."

Every nerve, every muscle in my body sparked with lightning at her words. *Even if the worst thing happens...*

The worst thing has already happened, Amma, I wanted to tell her. *It's you.*

Instead, with a new fire in my belly, I pulled my

phone from the pocket of my apron and opened up to a picture of us, my hand shaking as I turned it around. "This is him."

"Hm?" She was focusing on a new spot of dried soda on the red tile as she said it.

"This is my husband," I said again, finally drawing her attention back to me. Her eyes narrowed, focusing on the picture, then widened. "Joe."

She met my eyes only once, then covered her mouth and dropped the mop with an earth-shattering *crack*.

"Everything alright?" I feigned ignorance.

"I'm... I'm sorry... I—" She was ghastly white as she stared around in shock, her hands brushing each of the tables around us as if she were looking for something. She pointed to the phone again. "That's... That's your husband?"

"Yes, why?"

She moved past me, spinning around to wave a hand. "I'm sorry. I... I'm not feeling well. I need to..." She rushed into the break room, but just as I started to follow her, she reappeared in the dining room again with her coat and purse in hand. "I need to go. I'll call Jenna." With that, she dashed out the door, locking it behind her. I watched her through the glass windows, saw her eyes flick up to meet mine through the panes once more.

She'd seemed terrified when she left, and with good reason.

Perhaps she hadn't known the truth about Joe before now, but there were no more excuses.

She knew everything.

She knew the truth.

Finally, we were getting somewhere.

CHAPTER TWENTY-SEVEN

I placed the test on the bathroom counter, my body filled with quivering, twitching muscles. Running my hands under the warm water, I waited, trying to make sense of the thoughts swirling through my head.

"Well?" Joe asked from behind me, his voice tight with stress.

"It takes a few minutes."

He puffed out a breath, sitting down on the edge of the bathtub, bouncing both knees up and down nervously. I dried my hands, resting my back against the wall across from him as I chewed my lips.

"It's going to be negative," he said firmly, trying to convince us both. "It has to be."

I shrugged a shoulder. "Would it really be the worst thing? I mean, we *are* married. I know it wasn't in the plans right now, but—"

"*Yes*. Yes, it would be the worst thing, Edie.

We're..." He stood, walking toward me and placing his hands on my shoulders. "We're barely treading water here. Every new bill buries us deeper. They're talking about budget cuts at the school, and I'm trying to help out my parents wherever I can. We just..." He blew a puff of air from his lips. "This is the last thing we need right now. You have to see that."

I pursed my lips. "I do see that, but Joe, no one's ever ready. If I am pregnant, we'll have to figure out a way to make it work. We always figure it out. You said so yourself."

"Don't say that..." He shook his head.

I folded my hands together in front of me, picking at the cuticle around my thumb. "What would you rather me say? I won't have an abortion if that's what you're thinking."

"I didn't suggest that you should."

"What, then? You're looking at me as if I can just will it away. If I'm pregnant, I'm keeping the baby. The timing isn't right, no. But we're married. We're stable. I can get a better job—"

"Doing what? You love what you do!"

"Really? No one loves working retail." I scoffed.

"You've been there forever."

"Because it's comfortable. I have seniority. But I could find something else. I could go into banking, or I could work reception for a doctor's office. I'd make more and have a better schedule anyway."

"It's not always just as simple as you finding a new

job... It would help, sure, but it wouldn't be a miracle cure for all our debt. And who's to say you could even get hired somewhere else?"

"I have a good résumé. Good references. Why wouldn't I?"

"I didn't say you wouldn't. It's just that... Well, it's hard to get on at places like that."

"Why are you looking for any reason in the world for this not to work? What if it could? What if we could make it work?" I pleaded.

He furrowed his brow, staring at me with disbelief. "Edith, three days ago, you couldn't even stand for me to touch you. Now you want to have a baby with me?"

"I'm not saying I *want* to have a baby. I'm just saying that if that's what's going to happen, we need to make the best of it. And you're the one who said we needed to move on. You're the one who took me away and tried to make everything better, said you couldn't stand to lose me—"

"I can't!"

"So then don't."

"What is that? An ultimatum?"

"No," I said, glancing at the sink and reaching for the test. He moved back as I held it out. "It's a question... Are you in this with me or not?"

"It's..."

"It's positive," I confirmed. "We're pregnant. But I meant what I said this morning. I won't make you do this with me if you can't."

He sank down, leaning over his knees. "But you're going to have it?"

"I've made up my mind."

His nod came slowly, and he was blinking back tears as he spoke. "Okay..."

"Okay? Okay, what?"

"I don't..." He stood back up, pacing the room. "I don't know. I just need to think. I've got to go."

"You're supposed to be staying with your parents tonight, aren't you?" It wasn't really a question. He stayed with his parents every Friday night. He wouldn't return until Monday afternoon. Which gave me a small window of time to figure out the rest of my plan.

"I should cancel..." He was already walking toward the door, though. We both knew he had no intention of canceling.

"No. Go ahead," I told him, and when he glanced over his shoulder, I nodded. "Honestly, it's fine. They need you. I'll be okay. I have to work most of the weekend anyway. It'll give us both time to clear our heads and think this through."

He seemed hesitant. "Are you sure?"

"Positive."

His stare was distant. As if he'd already left. "I wouldn't go if they weren't counting on me to be there. Dad needs help fixing a broken part of his fence, and... I mean, I'll just be a phone call away if anything happens or if you need me for anything."

"I know. I'll call you if I need you." *I won't.*

His bag was already packed in our bedroom, and he stopped by to pick it up on his way down the hall. He kissed my forehead at the door. "I just need time to process," he promised. "I'm not going anywhere. You know that." He meant figuratively, of course. Realistically, he was pulling the door open, ready to dart.

"I know." I kissed his lips briefly. "It's all going to be okay."

His gaze flicked to my belly. "It doesn't seem real."

I realized then the test was still in my hand. "I know. None of this does."

"I love you."

"I love you."

He stared at me a moment longer, then nodded. "I should go."

"I'll talk to you soon."

With that, he stepped out the door, taking a few steps down the sidewalk and toward the parking lot before turning away from me. When he had, I shut the door, bolting it behind me and dropping to the ground.

I stared at the test.

How was any of this possible?

I was going to be a mom?

As much of a front as I'd put on for my husband about feeling brave and ready, I recognized the cool dread spreading through me now. My chest constricted with sharp breaths, my hands icy.

It was no longer about Joe.

Now, the little life inside me meant more than either of us. More than what I wanted. More than what my heart longed for. I had to make different choices now. If not for me, then for them.

I pressed my back against the wood of the door with so much force I was sure it would break. I needed to pull myself together, needed to stop the tears from falling, and figure out what came next.

With a sharp inhale, I pushed up from the floor, drying my tears as I moved to the kitchen and tossed the test out, then made my way back into the bedroom. There was only one person in the world who could make me feel better at that point, so I dialed his number quickly.

"Hi, honey, what's up?" he answered, all in one breath.

"Can you come over?"

"Um, in a heartbeat. Why? What happened? Are you *crying?*" In an instant, I could hear him shuffling around his apartment.

"I'm..." If I hadn't already been crying, I definitely was then, as I tried to force out the words I needed to tell my best friend.

"You're...what? Sick? Summering in France and want me to be your plus-one? Leaving Joe? A million-aire? Madly in love with me?" He laughed. "Come on, you're *what?* You're scaring me!"

"I'm pregnant," I said as I heard the rattle of his keys.

The movement on his end of the line stopped so abruptly I thought for a moment maybe we'd gotten disconnected. "Oh my god..."

"I don't know what to do."

The movement was back. I heard his keys, the sound of the door shutting, and the sound of wind through the phone letting me know he was outside. "Well, yeah. Are you...okay? Do you need me to stop and pick anything up? Wine or...well, probably not wine. Cookies? Ice cream?"

"No, nothing. I just want you to get here."

"I'll be walking in the door in five minutes, okay?" he said, and I was sure he was right, though he lived fifteen minutes away. I heard the car starting up, relief hitting me at knowing he was on the way.

I choked back sobs, pressing the phone to my ear harder. "Let it out, honey," he said. "Just let it out."

He kept me on the line as I cried, releasing sobs he couldn't yet understand. I was broken, cracked open, and torn down until it seemed as if there was nothing left inside of me. It felt like I might die from the pain I was in, though to anyone looking at me, I knew I appeared to be fine.

Everything hurt.

Everything felt terrifying.

There was no way around this. Any of it.

No more avoiding what was happening or pacing myself.

There was a very real timer on things now, and I had to act faster.

Be smarter.

Stronger.

This was about the baby. It had nothing to do with me or what I wanted anymore.

"Have you told Joe? I mean, it *is* Joe's, isn't it?" he asked when I'd gone silent for a while.

"Of course it's Joe's."

"I'm just saying I wouldn't blame you if it wasn't."

I shook my head. "It's Joe's. And yes, I told him."

"And what did he say?"

"He left to go to his parents."

He scoffed. "Have I told you lately how much I love him?"

I did my best to stifle my smile beneath my tears. "Once or twice."

His sigh was genuine, shifting the conversation from playful to serious. "How are you feeling? Are we happy or sad about this?"

"I don't know," I told him. "I mean, I'm not happy. It wasn't planned, you know? But I'm not really sad about it, either. I'm...scared. Very scared."

"Sure... That's certainly within reason."

"But it's not like I don't want kids. Maybe I didn't want them yet, but I could make it work."

"Of course you can. You absolutely can." I heard the car shut off through the line. "Okay, I'm here. Come let me in."

I met him at the door, doing a double take when I saw his appearance. One half of his face was done in full glam—glittery red eyeshadow and false lashes, a perfect contour, and a red lip. It was better makeup than I'd be able to apply on my best day. He held up a hand, stopping me before I said anything. "Don't you dare. I was in the middle of recording a new video for my channel when you called. I'm such a good friend I didn't waste time wiping it off."

I smiled at him through my tears. "Thank you."

He hugged me then, letting me collapse in his arms, and I let the tears fall freely as he rubbed my back. We stood there, right in the doorway, for minutes on end as I fell apart in my best friend's arms.

He rocked me and held me, brushing my hair from my damp cheeks and listening to my sobs as I tried to form coherent sentences.

When I'd calmed myself down, I slipped out of the hug, drying my eyes. There were tear stains on his beige sweater that instantly made me feel guilty.

"Don't worry about it. It'll wash. It's not the worst thing it's had on it, believe me," he said, following my gaze. "Now, let's go to the bathroom so I can wash this off, and you can tell me everything."

He led the way, scrubbing his face as I recounted the first suspicions that I might be pregnant, confronting Amma, and the positive pregnancy test.

When I was done, and his face was clean, he stared

at me sympathetically, processing all I'd told him. "So, what do you want to do?"

"I want to stay with him," I admitted. "But only if I can trust him."

"And *can* you?"

"I don't know."

"*I don't know* is not a good answer to that question," he said, following me as I led the way from the bathroom to our bedroom.

"I know. I looked all through his bank account, but I didn't see anything suspicious."

"Okay, well, that's a good thing. Where else did you check?" He sank down on the bed, his dark hair tumbling into his eyes.

"I checked his phone again. His social media and messages and photos all seemed okay, but...there was this app."

"The dating app you mentioned?" he asked, as if he already knew the answer.

"No. That was gone. No, it was called like...a vault app or something?" His eyes widened.

"What? Like one of the ones where you hide things inside, and they're meant to look like something else?"

"Yeah, exactly. Have you heard of them?"

"Heard of them? Honey, I *use* one like my life depends on it!"

"You do?" I asked, feeling shocked. "What? *Why?* Why would you need one?"

He fanned himself with his shirt. "Psshh... You

should see some of the dirty-birdy pictures Nick sends me. I can't just have those floating around on my phone for ole Barbara down at the mini-mart to stumble onto when I'm trying to find a screenshot of my coupons!" he teased.

"So, that's what you use it for? To hide photos?"

"Yes, why? What was he using it for?" He tilted his head to the side.

"I don't know. I didn't get a chance to ask him. I found it in the middle of the night and tried to open it..."

"Did you get inside?"

"No, I tried three times, and it deleted the app."

He nodded, obviously expecting I'd say that. "Yeah, that's what they do. But all of the information is saved. It'll go into a new app on his phone. And they usually send a snapshot of whoever was trying to access it to his email. So, I'm guessing he knows you tried to access it?"

"What?" My breathing quickened. "No. No. What? I didn't know that."

"He didn't mention it?"

"No. He didn't say a word."

"Do you have access to his email? If it's anything like mine, the app takes a picture of your face and emails it when it self-destructs. So, he probably has proof you did it."

I turned to face the computer. "I think I can access his email. If he didn't change the password."

"Well, come on! Let's check. Maybe you can get to it before he sees the email."

"Maybe," I said, logging into our computer and opening the browser to our email site. I typed in his email address and password and held my breath.

"We're in," Dan said, patting my shoulder excitedly. I scrolled through the emails—mostly unopened promotions and the monthly school newsletter.

"There's nothing," I said, scrolling up and down once again. "Nothing."

His response was solemn. "So, he's either already seen and deleted it, or his app is different from the one I use." He fell silent, a hopeless expression on his face.

I turned back to the computer, pulling up Joe's online banking account.

"What are you doing?" he asked.

"I'm pulling up his bank account again. I want to go over it while I have some time to really see everything. You can help me."

He leaned closer, staring at the screen as I logged in.

The latest transaction was for gas, where he'd likely just filled up on the way out of town. Before that was a two dollar and ninety-nine cent charge I didn't recognize.

I paused.

"What is it?" Dan asked, watching me, then looking back at the screen. "What's BusyText?"

"I have no idea. I've never seen this charge before."

I checked back further in his history, then returned to the top. I opened a browser, searching for the company.

"It's a messaging service," Dan read aloud. "You pay a monthly fee, claim a phone number, and then you can call or text anyone from the app or website."

"What does that mean?" I shook my head.

"I have no idea." His tone was ominous. "Here, click on the website and see what we can find out."

I did, scrolling through a page that further described what their service was. "So, if Joe has this app on his phone, he can text anyone from a different number?"

"I guess so..." Dan was still reading. "But why? Why not just use the phone number you have? What? Is he prank calling people? Are we eleven?"

"Do you think that's what he was hiding in the vault app?"

He shrugged. "It's possible."

"There's a place to sign in," I said, pointing my cursor toward it. "Should I try?"

His jaw tightened, sweat beading at his hairline. "I mean, you have to now."

I scrolled to the top of the page, clicked on the box where it allowed you to sign in, and typed his email address. "I'll probably have to change his password..." I typed in a password, clicking submit and gasping. "Or...not. We're in."

"What an idiot," he grumbled.

"He probably never thought I'd find out about it, so he wasn't worried about using a strong password."

"Okay, whoa," he said as the messages began to load. My jaw dropped at the same time. There were so many messages, going back months and months, maybe years. More than one hundred pages of text logs.

"Well, the account definitely isn't new," he said plainly, gesturing to the calls and texts that went back months.

I dragged the cursor toward the center of the page. "There's my number." I clicked on it, reading through our conversations. They were innocent enough, so why were they hidden in an app? Why wasn't he just texting me from his number? Why hadn't I noticed that his number had been changed?

I reached for my phone at the end of the bed.

"What are you doing?" he asked.

Without answering, I pulled up my contacts, clicking on Joe's name. "It's this number..." I trailed off. "He changed his number in my phone to match the one in the app. I haven't even been talking to him on the phone number I pay for. Why would he do that?"

Dan's mouth wrinkled with pity. "Do you want to know my honest opinion?"

I nodded.

"If he has multiple phones, it's probably easier to text and call everyone through a single app. He signs on from anywhere and has access to everything."

I swallowed, the possibilities overwhelming. "Click

on the last messages he's sent," Dan instructed, turning back to study the screen.

I turned my focus back to the computer, clicking on the top few messages and reading through them quickly.

"Oh my god..." he whispered.

"It's her," I confirmed, breathless as I read through the conversation.

"Uh, yeah."

"This was from today," I told him, though we could both see the date.

The first message came from Amma around two, just four hours after our confrontation at the restaurant.

We need to talk.

His outgoing message said, **About what?**

I met Edith.

What are you talking about?

Edith. I met her today. How long have you been lying to me, Joe?

I don't know anyone named Edith.

Stop lying. She had a picture of the two of you together.

Oh! Wait, no, no... I didn't lie. I don't know how she found you or what she told you, but if you're talking about who I think you are, she's a liar. Whatever she told you, don't believe her.

I can't do this anymore, Joe.

Wait, please… Give me a chance to explain.

When she hadn't responded, he messaged her again, **Please answer your phone.**

Her response came quickly, **No.**

Look, Edith is…crazy. I don't use that term lightly. She's been in and out of care centers. She's delusional. She believes I love her, but I haven't seen or talked to her in years. I never told you about her because I didn't want to scare you. I have a restraining order out on her and everything.

It had been several minutes before she responded. **How is that possible? How do I know I can believe you?**

Whatever picture she had, it was from when we were together. Years ago. Way before I met you. Before I realized how messed up she is. You are all I could ever want. You know that. She's dangerous, okay? Just stay away from her. Can I come see you? Are you at work?

When she didn't answer, he'd said, **I'm leaving the school right now. I'll come see you. Please. Let's just talk about this in person.**

Amma? Please let me explain further in person. Please.

Are you at home?

Amma?

I read through the conversation twice, my eyes swimming with tears. When I looked at Dan, he appeared just as broken and at a loss for words as I felt.

He cleared his throat, speaking softly. "Honey, let's get your stuff and get out of here, okay?" He brushed the hair from my eyes. "You can't stay here another minute. I will drag you kicking and screaming if that's what I have to do."

I shook my head, my jaw tight. "You won't have to drag me."

"You don't deserve this," he said.

Cool tears gathered in my eyes as I nodded. "Can I stay with you?"

"For the rest of your life, if that's what you want. I've told you that. You always have a place with me. It'll be just like college." He slid his arm around my shoulder. "It's all going to be okay. We'll make sure of it."

I nodded again, sniffling. It was over, all over. And I was pregnant. I fought against the panic welling inside me. If I allowed myself to become consumed by it, I wouldn't leave this chair. I had things to do. I needed to be strong, if not for myself, then for this baby.

"How long is he gone? How long do we have?" Dan asked as he walked away from me, pulling out a suitcase.

"He'll be at his parents' house for the weekend, so we don't have to worry about him coming back until Monday. But the sooner we can get out, the better."

"Okay, good. Should I call in reinforcements? Nick can get a few of his friends over. We'll clean out the whole house if that's what you want."

I shook my head. "No, just a few of my things. Clothes, mostly. I don't want to... I just can't. Not yet. Eventually, maybe."

"Are you sure?" He studied me as if trying to remind me this was my one and only chance, but I wouldn't change my mind about this. I couldn't. I just needed enough to last a few days, and then I needed to get the hell out of this house before I suffocated with grief. "Okay," he said finally. "Tell me what to pack." He'd already begun digging through my drawers, tossing entirely too many things into the bag as I tried to pull myself together. Once he'd emptied my side of the dresser, he moved on to digging through the closet. "Anything in here you want to take? Sentimental stuff or...?" He trailed off when he caught my eyes.

"Why didn't I see it sooner, Dan?" I begged, sniffling. "Why did I keep trusting him?"

His bottom lip puckered with pity. "You had love blinders on, honey. Happens to the best of us."

I brushed tears from my eyes, standing up and

turning away from him. "What's in here? Anything you want to bring?"

When I looked behind me, Dan was digging through the old plastic tote where Joe kept old documents—manuals for our appliances, our lease agreement, Christmas and birthday cards from years past.

"Junk," I said dryly. "Stuff we don't have use for, but Joe refuses to throw away. The thing gives me hives, but he swears we might need it someday. That's why it's hidden back there—out of sight, out of mind."

"Awww. Pictures from our trip to Florida after graduation," he said, pulling out a stack of photos and flipping through them with a nostalgic smile on his face. He gave a subdued laugh. "Look at those tan lines."

"Really? Our graduation trip?" My brows shot up as I made my way toward the closet in search of the key from Joe's suitcase. I wanted to look through the drawers again in case there was anything else in there I might want. "I didn't realize he put those in there. No wonder I couldn't find them."

"Hey, who are Ada and Edwin?"

I spun around, trying to see what he was talking about. "Huh?"

He held up two pieces of paper. "Ada and Edwin Anderson?"

"They're Joe's parents... What are those?"

His eyes widened as he met mine. "Are you sure?"

"Why wouldn't I be?" I tried to get a better look at the papers in his hand.

His expression was grim as he handed over the documents, my blood chilling as I realized what I was staring at. "Because these death certificates say Joe's parents, the ones he's supposed to be staying with right now, died a year ago."

CHAPTER TWENTY-EIGHT

"Are you sure this is a good idea?" Dan asked as we pulled into Amma's subdivision.

"If his parents are dead, then he's not staying with them, obviously. It means every time he's told me that's where he's going, he's been staying somewhere else. When he left me while we were staying at the hotel, he went somewhere else. You read those messages, same as I did. He wanted to see her. I'll bet anything he's here. He has to be here. Has to be with her."

"Look, I am all fired up for this *vigilante, kicking ass and taking names* version of my best friend. I just want to know what exactly your plan is."

"I don't know if I have one," I said, turning down her street. "I just have to know."

"To know what? To know that your husband is an asshole? You already know that. To know that he's lying to this woman about you? You already know that.

To know that he's lied to you about everything, including his own parents' deaths for your entire marriage? I'm sorry, babe. But you know that, too."

"Look, I know it doesn't make any sense. Trust me, I get it. But I need to know. I just do. And he's never going to be honest with me. The only way to get the truth out of him is to catch him with her, in person."

"But you saw the messages. She was ignoring him. Do you really think he just came over here?"

"I don't know what to think. But if he's not here, where else could he be?"

"I just think you deserve better than this. Just...just walk away from it. Walk away and be happy. Forget him. Divorce him and be happy again. You don't need him, Edith. I wish you could see that."

"I know I don't need him. I do. I just..." I sniffled again, looking out the window. "I need to do this for me. I don't know why, but it's what I need. I know you think it's crazy. That I'm crazy—"

"You aren't crazy," he snapped. "Don't you ever let him put that in your head."

I licked my lips, nodding solemnly.

He sighed, running a hand over his face. "Okay, you know what? Screw it. Let's do this."

"Yeah?"

He clapped his hands. "Yeah. Let's go. I don't have any plans. If this dude wants to talk about crazy, let's show him crazy."

I was too nervous to laugh at his joke as we

rounded the curve, and I laid eyes on her house. It was dark in the neighborhood, but her porch light was on, and a single window was lit up in the otherwise dark house. "That's it."

"I'm scared to know how you know this."

"I followed her," I said, too tired to find a better, less honest way to explain it.

"Well, that'll do it. It doesn't look like anyone's home. Joe's car isn't here."

"She's married. Maybe her husband leaves for work, and Joe comes over after. But either way, I don't think they'd leave his car in the open. The neighbors might see it and start asking questions. If her husband is gone, maybe Joe's car is parked in their garage." I gripped the wheel tighter, trying to come to terms with my next move. "There's only one way to find out."

"What? You mean go look? You know we live in the South, right? People have guns here. Gun collections. Gun-shaped display cases to show off their gun collections."

"Well, don't worry. You can stay here. Keep the car running in case we have to make a break for it."

"No way. I'm kidding. I'll go with you."

He was already unbuckling, but I held up a hand to stop him.

"It's fine, Dan, honestly. Stay here. I can't put you in danger. I'd never forgive myself. And it does make sense to have a getaway driver, no matter how unreliable his driving record." I elbowed him playfully, but this time, he didn't smile.

"If you expect me just to sit here and wait while you—"

"That's exactly what I expect. If I'm on that side of the garage, I won't be able to see the house. You can switch sides with me, though, and stay here. Keep an eye out and call my phone if you see anyone. I'm just going to look in the window for his car."

He inhaled deeply. "Alright."

I opened the car door as he did the same, and we rotated seats. As he slid into the driver's seat, I leaned down from the passenger side. "I'll be right back." I was breathless, my muscles tense as I prepared to run.

"Go. Hurry up," he said when I hesitated. "Before someone sees."

"Right." I turned, glancing over my shoulder at the garage and moving to shut the door.

As I did, he shouted, "Wait!"

I leaned back down. "Yeah?"

At the same time, he said, "Do you hear that?"

I couldn't hear anything over the sound of my racing heart, but I followed his line of vision just in time to see the lights in the distance—flashing red and blue. A warning. The police were on their way.

"Do you think she called the cops on us?" he asked. "Do you think she saw us?"

I cast a glance at the house, spying the silhouette of someone in the lighted window. She was watching us.

"Shoot. We should go," I told him, my mouth suddenly too dry.

"You don't have to tell me twice." I was in the car, attempting to buckle as he sped off, exiting the street moments before the police cruiser pulled into the subdivision.

It took several minutes before I realized the trembling I felt wasn't entirely coming from my body. I reached in my pocket, pulling out my buzzing phone. I'd expected to see Amma, but instead, Joe's name was on my screen.

"He's calling me," I told Dan, my voice breathless.

"Don't you dare answer," he said, gripping the wheel with both hands.

"You don't have to tell me twice," I dryly repeated the line he'd just said, placing my phone down.

What did he want?

Why was he calling?

The questions would have to remain just that for a while longer. Questions.

My husband was running out of secrets, and soon, I'd know the truth about them all.

CHAPTER TWENTY-NINE

The next morning, when I left the house, I had to promise a worried Dan I wouldn't be gone long. He'd wanted to come with me, but there were some things I needed to handle alone.

My phone was off, sick of Joe's incessant calling, sick of my own disgusting desire to answer it.

I'd hardly slept the night before, and I was in no mood to do anything at all, but I owed Jenna more of a courtesy than that. Which was why quitting my job in person was first on my to-do list.

I hated that this was what it had come to. I'd always known I wouldn't stay at this job for long, but I'd hoped to be able to give her proper notice at least. As it stood, I couldn't bear to work there another day. Couldn't bear to go back to the place that would always be filled with such terrible memories for any stretch of time. But this, this one small kindness, I did owe to the boss who'd made my life just a small bit more endurable lately.

I walked into the restaurant. I wasn't scheduled to come in until one, so when Jenna saw me, I watched her face fill with confusion. She glanced at the schedule on the wall, then back at me as I neared the counter.

"Edith? We weren't expecting you yet... Are you feeling better?"

I shook my head, touching my stomach warily. "Not really."

"I hate that you and Amma came down with something on the same day."

"I'm not contagious," I told her, not bothering to explain. "But I'm actually here to talk to you, if you have a minute."

Her lips pursed, her face telling me she already knew what I was planning to do. Her shoulders fell with disappointment, and when she tried to smile, it was obviously forced. "You're not quitting, are you?"

"I'm..." A few of the staff were milling around behind her, visibly trying to listen in. "I'm so sorry. I have to. It's nothing you've done. I love working here. It's just that my circumstances have changed, and this doesn't work for me anymore. You've been the best boss, and I hate this. If there were any other way..." I trailed off.

"I understand, but we hate to see you go. Do you want to talk about this more in my office? Maybe we can figure something out?" She was trying to figure me out, to understand what had changed, but I was a fortress today, impenetrable even to those I cared about most.

"I don't think so. It's just—" I was interrupted by the sound of the small metal bell above the entrance. When I looked over, my heart leaped into my throat. Joe narrowed his gaze at me, his face ashen.

"Edith?" He looked around, as if in shock, then shook his head.

"What are you doing here?" I asked, unable to care about who was around. Tears welled in my eyes. *So much for my fortress.* "Did you follow me?"

"Edith, is everything alright?" Jenna asked, keeping her voice low. "Do you need me to call the police?" Her hand grazed my arm.

"It's alright." I waved off her concern. Joe had moved closer to me then, his eyes scanning the restaurant.

"What are *you* doing here?" he demanded. "I've been trying to call you all night. I've been worried sick." He pulled me into his arms, hugging me tightly, and I realized then that he was crying.

I eased myself out of his hug. "I'm sorry," I whispered, saying it more to Jenna than Joe. "We should go. Let's talk outside."

"Call me, okay?" Jenna said. "If you need anything. Or if you change your mind." She watched us as we made our way out of the restaurant, my stomach filled with sorrow at the thought of leaving someone who seemed to care so much about me. Maybe she was the only person I had, besides Dan, who did.

Once outside, Joe stared me up and down, as if checking me for injuries. "Where have you been? I've been driving all over town. You weren't at home last night. I tried calling you... I called the store this morning, and they told me you're on leave?" He gave a dry laugh as if it were ridiculous. "That's... I mean, that's not true, is it? It can't be. I would've noticed... You would've told me..." He was trailing off, waiting for me to answer the questions he wasn't directly asking.

"I took leave from the store a few weeks ago, yes. I've been working here."

"Here?" he asked, his brows bouncing up with surprise. "Why?"

"Don't you know that? That's why you're here, right?"

"Well, yeah, but not because I thought you worked here... Or, well, I guess I did. I didn't know what to think. When they told me you were on leave, I thought maybe you'd just asked them to say that. I drove to the shop, and you really weren't there. I was driving home when I saw your car across the street, and I just... I saw you walking in. I didn't know what I was going to do or say. I just needed to get to you. I was so scared I'd lost you..."

I sucked in a sharp breath, cutting him off. "Just cut the crap, Joe. I know about everything, okay?"

"Everything?" He furrowed his brow.

"Yeah, everything. I know about your affair. I know you told her I'm crazy and that we aren't together and you haven't seen or talked to me in months—"

"What are you talking about?" he asked, his eyes wide, hands on either side of his head. "You're not making any sense, Edith. Are you hearing yourself right now? Who did I tell that you're crazy? Of course I've seen you. Of course we're together. We're *married*, for Christ's sake. Where is any of this coming from?"

I pulled out my phone, angry and frustrated, and opened the BusyText app I'd downloaded last night with the messages I'd spent an embarrassing number of hours reading through. I shoved it toward him. "How can you lie your way out of this? I know about Amma. Sam was never behind the pictures, okay? I've figured it all out. I know about your little app. The one you've been hiding and using to text us. I know about the vault app, too, the one you were probably trying to hide the pictures in. I know what you said to her." I gestured toward the phone. "All of this horrible, nasty stuff about me. What I don't know is why... Why would you put either of us through this? If you want to be with her so much, just go!" I fought back tears as I said it. "Just go. Please. Just leave me alone."

He was struggling to read the messages as I shook from crying, but once he had, his expression crinkled with confusion. "Edith, I don't know what any of this is, but I swear to you, I never sent those messages. I don't have...did you say *vault app?* I have no idea what that even means. I have no idea who Amma is. And I'd never talk about you this way." He pointed at the phone. "Look, let's just calm down, alright? There's something I want to tell you, and it has nothing to do with any of this. I left last night, but I shouldn't have. You'd just told me you were pregnant, and instead of staying and talking things out, I ran. I ran like a coward, and I hated myself for it. I stayed at Mom and Dad's for a few hours before it ate me up, and I turned right around and came home. But you weren't there. I haven't slept a wink. I was on the verge of going to the cops. But I saw your bag was gone. I knew you'd left me. I just didn't know why. I—"

"You went to your parents' house last night?" I asked, not buying another minute of his lies.

"Yeah, of course I did. I told you I did."

"You're still lying to me!"

"I'm not—"

"I know your parents are dead, Joe!" I screamed, my voice echoing through the quiet street. An elderly man who'd been sitting on a bench nearby stood, hurrying away from us with haste.

His face went ghastly white, his jaw slack, and I waited for him to argue. But he didn't. To my surprise, he just stood there, his brows raised, blinking back tears.

Finally, he hung his head, covering his face with his palms. "I'm so sorry."

"You've been lying to me all this time."

"I haven't..."

I turned to walk away. "I don't have time for this."

"Please just—" He grabbed my arm, trying to stop me. "Please let me explain. You'll understand it all if you'll just give me a chance."

"I've given you plenty of chances, Joe. And you've lied or made me feel crazy or told other people I'm crazy. I'm done trying to understand you. I'm done feeling like I've done something wrong. I'm done judging myself for not being enough for you when, in all reality, whatever you've got going on runs so much deeper than just us. I can't be with you anymore, Joe. I'm leaving you. I want a divorce. You can keep the apartment, or sublet it, or whatever... I'll take care of the baby. You don't have to have anything to do with it. I just want out. I can't do this anymore." I sobbed openly, rushing across the street and toward my car as he fought to keep up with me.

"You won't even let me explain? You'll really throw all of this away for—"

I spun around, my arms rigid at my sides. "*You had a chance to explain!* You've had a year to explain, and all you've ever done is lie."

"It's..." He stammered, "Well, i-it's not that simple."

"Of course it is." I reached for my keys.

"Please, Edith, please. I can't lose you." He grabbed hold of my arm, and I jerked it away again.

KIERSTEN MODGLIN

"Just leave me alone. Okay? Do you hear me? Leave me alone. Go home. Or go stay with your girlfriend. Or stay wherever else you've been staying, but leave me alone. Don't call. Don't text—"

"Where will you go—"

"It doesn't matter anymore."

"Of course it matters. You're pregnant with my child. I have a right to know you're safe—"

When he grabbed my arm this time, I whirled around, smacking him square on the cheek. I hadn't meant to do it, hadn't even realized I was going to until it happened. I covered my mouth, breathing frantically. "Don't you dare try to use this baby against me. Not ever. *Not ever, Joe.* Just leave me alone."

He cupped a hand over his cheek, checking his palm as if he thought there might be blood on it. "I can't believe you're doing this..." he whispered breathlessly.

"I need time, okay? I need space. I need a chance to work through all of this, and I can't—" I pulled open the car door. "I can't look at you right now."

"I don't want that." He was sobbing, openly weeping as he watched me climb into the car. "Please... I don't want this. Please, Edith, just talk to me. You don't have to be with me, but please just talk to me."

He wanted me to react, to see his tears and move to comfort him as I always had, but I wouldn't. I couldn't. He was a liar. A cheater. A manipulator. I needed to keep moving if I had any hope of getting out of the mess he'd put me in. If I took long enough, if I listened to the heartbreak happening inside of me, I'd make a mistake. I'd take him back, and we'd move on. Until the next time. And the next.

I couldn't do that.

I slammed the car door, locking it quickly and starting it up. I worried he'd try to stop me as I pulled away, but he didn't. Instead, he stood, crying in the snow that had begun to fall, his cheeks red from the cold and the tears. I didn't look back, not as I turned the car out of the parking lot and not as I merged left rather than turning right.

I wasn't going to Dan's apartment just yet.

I needed to make a pit stop at a gray house in a busy subdivision across town.

CHAPTER THIRTY

As I was leaving Amma's subdivision a few hours later, my phone buzzed with an incoming call from Dan.

"Hello?"

"Hey, everything okay?"

"Yeah..." I hesitated.

"Where are you?"

I winced, unsure how I wanted to tell him about the stupid things I'd done. "I went back to her house."

He gasped. I could picture him pacing the floor of his apartment, no place to defuse his anger. "You what? Why would you do that? What happened? What did she say? What did you say? Oh my god! *You what?*"

"Nothing. Just breathe. I didn't talk to her. I just drove by. It's fine. Oh, and I officially left Joe."

"Uh, yeah, I was there, remember?"

"No, I mean, I told him I left him and everything. He came by the restaurant—"

"Wait, he found out you worked there?"

"No, he was looking for me at the store and just happened to see me going into the restaurant, I guess. But anyway, he said he felt guilty about storming out last night after I told him about the baby—"

"As he should."

"Right, and so he said he was calling last night because he came home to tell me how sorry he was. But, of course, I wasn't there. So, apparently, he's been all over town looking for me and calling me."

He let out a *hmph*. "Serves him right."

"Anyway, I told him I knew everything. About the other phone and the text messages and Amma and his parents."

He inhaled sharply. "*And?* What did he say?"

"Nothing, really. He just said there's more to it. Well, first, he tried to lie, actually. He said he didn't have a fake phone, and the messages weren't from him. But when I asked him about his parents, there was nothing else he could do. He knew he was caught. So, he started crying—"

"Of course he did."

"And he begged me for a chance to explain—"

"Which you did not give him..."

"No, I did not. I told him I want a divorce. I told him to leave me alone, that I needed time."

"And he agreed?"

"Well, he wasn't happy about it, but I didn't give him a choice. I just drove away and left him there."

"Yes, you did!" He clapped.

"But then I went to Amma's for two reasons."

"I would love to hear them."

"One, she wasn't at work today, and I'm sure she was on the schedule, so I wanted to check and make sure she was okay after we saw the police nearby last night. I was worried something bad may have happened..."

"And what did you find out?"

"She was fine. I mean, like I said, I didn't talk to her. But I saw her outside with her daughter."

"Okay, so what was the other reason?"

"I wanted to see if Joe would come to her house after I'd left him."

"And did he?"

"No," I said, shaking my head, though he couldn't see me. "No. I sat nearby for half an hour. Plenty of time for him to have gotten there. But he didn't come. I would've stayed longer if I wasn't worried the neighbors would start to get suspicious."

"You should've come and gotten me. You know I'm excellent on a stakeout."

"Mhm," I said dryly. "As I saw last night."

He chuckled. "Okay, so are you coming back here now? I was just about to grab lunch."

"No, I need to run by the apartment first. There

are a few more things I want to get now that things are more permanent."

"Want me to come with you?"

"Nah, I'll be okay. It'll be quick."

"What if he's there?"

"If I know Joe at all, which is questionable these days, I don't think he'll be there. My guess is he's probably out trying to find me or chase down Amma. But if he is, I'll leave. I'm not in a place to confront him again today."

"Okay, well, be careful, alright? And call me if you need anything. You're coming straight back here after, aren't you?"

"Yep, that's the plan."

"Text me if it changes."

"Okay, mom," I teased.

"Honey, someone has to be your mom right now. 'Cause you've got a badass boyfriend who's taking you down a very dark road. Momma's gotta fix it all."

I grinned, despite the overwhelming sadness. "Okay, I'll talk to you soon. Love you."

He made a kissing noise through the phone before we disconnected, leaving me alone in the silent car. Normally, riding so long in silence would be pure torture. I preferred to put on concerts as I drove, singing pop songs from the playlists on my phone at full blast, including my own backup vocals, but today wasn't a concert sort of day.

Today was about sadness.

About saying goodbye.

About accepting what I hadn't been able to for so long and moving forward.

Today was about the end of everything I'd known and being brave enough to take the first step into my future—whatever it looked like.

CHAPTER THIRTY-ONE

I was staring at my phone screen, at the latest message to come through the BusyText app from Joe's account to Amma's phone. A lump had grown in my throat, dry and uncomfortable, my entire body too cold and too warm all at once.

I'd parked in our parking lot, preparing to go inside, when I saw Amma's bright-blue SUV. That was where she'd been going after she left her house.

Now, the message sat there, staring back at me.

Telling me why she was here. Now. In my parking lot.

Come see me. Please. There's so much to explain. Just give me a chance. 105 North Franklin Road Apt 201. I'll be here all night.

Amma was still in her vehicle. I could stop her. I could rush up to her and beg her to leave. Would she listen? I didn't know.

But I couldn't. I had to let this play out. It was the only way.

I watched her exit her SUV. No longer was she the cheery woman I'd met at Jenna's. She looked worn down now. Her eyes were puffy and red, even from a distance.

This was what Joe did to people.

This was how he destroyed us.

I opened my car door, slipping out and following close behind her. Close enough I could see where she was going but not so close as to draw attention to myself.

She made her way under the covered sidewalk into the breezeway that led to our apartment with ease. She'd been here before. There was no looking around or searching for apartment numbers. She walked straight to the door like she belonged there.

When she'd reached it, she looked back over her shoulder.

Straight at me.

Then she smiled.

CHAPTER THIRTY-TWO

I pushed open the door to the apartment and stepped into the dimly lit living room.

Joe sat up, a beer bottle in his hand. He swiped his hand across his cheek, staring at me with confusion, then relief. "You...came home?" He moved to stand, but I put up a hand, stopping him.

"I won't be here long."

"I know you're angry with me, but if you'll just listen..."

The door opened again, and we both turned as Amma entered. "Listen to what, Joe?"

"Amma?" he asked, his voice hollow sounding, as if the life had drained from his body in a second.

"Who do you want to explain it to first, hm?" she asked, crossing her arms. Despite the tears in her eyes, she held firm, staring at him with a look of pure disgust.

A sheepish expression crossed his face, and he

pointed between us. "What is this? What's going on? How do the two of you know each other?"

"Oh, us? We're old pals, didn't you know?" I sneered.

"The wife and the mistress, who would've thought..." Amma added, the corners of her lips upturned.

"It's not like that—" he said, only he wasn't talking to me, wasn't trying to explain it all to me anymore.

"Oh, I know it's not. Edith's told me all about what it's *like*... All about how you let her believe *I* was the other woman?" she spat, her nostrils flaring as she turned up her nose at him.

His gaze flicked to me, but I held firm. I wasn't going to show the shock I'd felt the day before when I'd learned the truth.

"I..." He tried to think quickly, but at the end of the day, he just wasn't that smart. "Look, this is all a misunderstanding."

"No, it's not," Amma said simply. "See, two days ago, Edith here was telling me all about how she was pregnant and nervous because the father of her baby didn't seem to want it. And, of course, because I'd been in that situation myself, I couldn't help feeling sorry for her and trying to offer some advice." Her upper lip curled with revulsion. "What I should've said was run — Run as far and as fast as you can. It's what I should've done all those years ago."

"You don't mean that..." He was pivoting between

us, attempting to keep his eyes on us both as he tried to determine which fire to put out first.

"Oh, I really do, Joe. You have no idea how much I do." She cocked her hip. "Anyway, when she showed me a picture of her husband, you can imagine my surprise when the man she showed me was also *my* husband."

The room shifted, a swift, dizzying sensation filling my belly. Sweat gathered on my forehead, and I resisted the urge to wipe it away. Even knowing the truth, hearing it out loud again, hearing the confirmation once more, only made me feel more light-headed.

Angry.

Bitter.

Devastated.

Everything I'd believed about my life was a lie.

I'd chased her down the street after she stormed out, thinking I knew what the hell was going on. "I know why you're running," I'd shouted after her. "What would Phillip think if he knew?"

Her face had changed from anger to confusion in an instant. "Phillip? My brother? What does he have to do with anything?"

From there, she'd imploded my whole world, telling me about how her brother had moved from Cleveland to live with them and help take care of their daughter when they couldn't afford childcare. How he'd bought their house for them. He could run his business from anywhere, and Dale was apparently just as good a place as any. And since her husband could only stay at home half the week thanks to his parents' declining health, she'd needed her brother's help more than ever.

"Okay, look," Joe said, sucking in a breath. "Yes, you caught me." He laughed. "I don't really know what else to say. You caught me. But you have to believe me when I tell you I never meant to hurt either of you."

"Well, you'll have to believe us"—she wagged a finger between us—"when we tell you that line doesn't really mean a whole lot right now."

She took a step toward me. "When Edith showed me the picture, all I could do was flash back to all the other times you've cheated, Joe. All the times you've lied. All the times I've caught you. All the therapy. We just kept gluing our marriage back together, time and time again, just forcing the pieces back together, trimming them up here and there, bending the corners when we needed to make something fit, and then... when she told me, when she showed me—the puzzle pieces finally snapped."

She held her hands out, wiggling her fingers as if her palms had exploded. "And I realized there was no more gluing us back together. No more bent edges or trimmed pieces. No more forcing things to work when they so clearly don't. Not when a random girl I work with can be your latest affair. Or my hairdresser. Or my best friend."

She put her hands over her face, expelling a loud

sigh. When she pulled away, there were fresh tears in her eyes. "I tried to run. I couldn't break down at work. All I could think about was little Zoe at home, thinking her daddy is the greatest thing in the world."

That, maybe more than anything else, seemed to break him. His chin quivered. "You know how much I love her..."

Amma wasn't done. "I would never want this marriage for our child, Joe." She placed a hand on her stomach. "Our children."

"But when she ran away, I couldn't let her go," I explained, speaking up finally. "She rushed out of the building, and I called our boss to let her know we were both sick. I finally had my chance to get answers, answers I'd been searching for for a long time, and I wasn't going to let them get away from me again."

"And so I told her everything," Amma said plainly.

"How you've been married for ten years. How you have a daughter. A home. A life."

"And Edith told me how you met her three years ago and married her a year later. Right around the time Zoe was born." Venom dripped from her tone. "Your parents wanted to live in the South, so you moved us here, moved us away from my family, to this state I've always hated, and you got a girlfriend six months later."

"I never intended for it to happen..."

"*No,*" she snapped, wagging a finger at him violently, her face pinched and red. "You don't get to say that, Joe. You can *not intend* to spill your drink at dinner. You can *not intend* to pick up the wrong brand of cereal at the grocery store. You can *not intend* to wash my new red dress with our white clothing and stain everything pink. What you can't do is accidentally get a girlfriend, lie to her about your family, and then marry her. You're a bigamist! A cheater, a liar, and a fucking bigamist, Joe! Don't you get that? And now the two of us, our lives are all turned upside down because you had to have your cake and eat it, too." Her cheeks flushed brighter red as she shouted, her eyes growing even wider as her fury swelled.

He sank down on the couch, his head in his hands.

"What were you thinking?" I asked him, my voice soft. "What did you think was going to happen with all of this?"

"I wasn't thinking," he said bluntly. "I loved you both. Don't scoff," he warned Amma when she did. "It's true. I did. I loved you, Amma. And I was happy with you. But I wanted something...different. I don't know. It sucks. I get it. But people do it, right? People have open marriages and sister wives and all of that—"

"Not without everyone's consent, you asshole!" she shouted, stomping a foot. She was beginning to get loud enough I worried my neighbors might hear. Then again, it wasn't as if fights were uncommon in our complex. I was sure they'd just turn their TV up louder to drown us out.

He winced at the volume of her shouting, then looked at me, obviously trying to calm us down as he lowered his tone, speaking casually as if we were at a dinner party and just catching up. "How did you two even find each other, anyway? Is that why you asked for leave? You started working at Amma's restaurant to tell her about me?"

"Oh, no!" Amma shouted. "You don't get to ask the questions around here. We'll be the ones asking—"

"I knew—er, well, I *thought* I knew—you were having an affair when I found the pictures on your phone—"

"Which I told you weren't mine."

"No, they were mine," Amma said firmly. Joe's eyes widened, though mine did not. Amma and I had already discussed all of this and more when I spoke with her at her house after we left work yesterday. Anything that hadn't been covered then had been discussed today when I went back to talk to her after seeing Joe outside the restaurant.

"When I discovered the charges for the texting app on our account, I started going through your phone. Only, I couldn't find it. The only text messages I could ever find were from your coworkers. Even the texts I sent you never appeared in your messages. I'm assuming your coworkers kept your original number because you never had access to their phones to change it... Or maybe it was just too hard to get everyone to change over? Anyway, I knew you well enough to know what that meant. If you were hiding it from me, it meant you were hiding so much else, too. But you'd never just be a man and admit what you were up to. You never had."

She paced the room, her tone flat. "I knew I needed to catch you in the act. So, that's what I set out to do. But I had to be smart about it, right? You know all the usual tricks. All the ways I've caught you before. No, this time, it had to be something better. I had to call in someone much smarter than I am."

She paused, smiling at him before continuing. "Of course, Phil was the perfect person to help me. He's smart, you know? Techy, right? And oh, he hates you for what you've done to his baby sister. His team created a program that could piggyback on any other app—like, say, a dating app?"

She winked at me. "So, it looked like you had a dating app on your phone, and you did, but really, the tracker was there, too. Working diligently in the background. Once we'd downloaded it onto your phone, you could still use the dating app like it was intended, but the tracker was there, silently detecting your every move. And when you deleted the dating app, the tracker stayed put because I was the only one who could disable it within the program." She smiled cruelly.

"I saw you coming to the address, staying at *this* address. Obviously, I couldn't see what apartment you were in, but I followed you one night and saw you coming here. I saw which apartment you entered. I knew what was going on, knew you were having an affair. So, then, when I saw you at the hotel, on a night when you'd normally be here, I planned to come here and confront her. To confront whatever woman you'd chosen this time. I knew confronting *you* wouldn't do any good. I've done that too many times, but nothing ever changes. And I knew that meant I had to leave, but first, I was going to warn her. I was going to tell her that you would destroy her, just like you'd destroyed me. On the way over here, I called you to tell you the jig was up. I told you I knew about the affair and that I was leaving you."

"So, you abandoned me at the hotel to go and search for her," I said, revealing what we'd been able to piece together. "But you couldn't find her because she wasn't at the house. She was here. At our apartment."

"Only when I got here, the place was dark. There was a key lying on the mat, and I was so angry, I wasn't thinking straight... I knocked on the door and, when no one answered, I came inside. Maybe I just wanted to see her. To see whatever life you'd built here. But, when I got inside, I heard someone moving around in another room, and I panicked. I wasn't willing to go to jail over you. You weren't worth that, no matter how furious I was with you. So, I bolted." She shook head, pinching the bridge of her nose.

"So, when I told you there was someone in the apartment, you lied and told me it was your dad," I said.

"And you called me to tell me the apartment was a

place for you to decompress when things got *too bad*."
She rolled her eyes. "You really are a good liar, you
know that?"

"So good you've planned for everything," I added.
"See, I downloaded the texting app. I've gone through
your messages there. It's clever, actually, the fact that
you've got us all named 'Mom' in your contacts. So, if
anyone calls you, you have a chance to get away, and
we're none the wiser. You really thought of
everything."

"Pretty sick, though, isn't it?" Amma asked. "To use
your dead mother as a means to cheat on your wife
—*wives*." She shivered. "Anyway, I needed a new plan,
so I uploaded a few photos of myself onto your phone
next. I figured, if you found them, you'd start worrying
about how much access I had to your phone, you know,
make you sweat a little...or, if nothing else, you'd realize
how smokin' hot your wife is and give up the stupid
games. And, well, I thought, if someone else found
them, maybe she'd at least start asking enough questions to scare you off."

"And I did. I found them," I said, finishing the
story. "But because I thought *I* was your wife, I
believed you were having an affair with her. I started
digging into who the woman was. I tried to Google you
like I did when we first met, but do you have any idea
how many Joe Andersons there are in the world?" I
paused. "I'm guessing you do, or this probably wouldn't
have gone on for as long as it did. It's why you could get

away with having multiple social media accounts, as long as you never showed your face in them."

I shook my head. "Anyway, so, when I was just about to give up hope, I thought I'd follow you one day when you were supposed to be going to your parents' house. I thought maybe, just maybe, I'd get lucky and catch you going and doing something you shouldn't have been." I narrowed my gaze. "Some*one* you shouldn't have been. I thought I'd have to follow you a few different times before you actually slipped up, but I should've known better. If there's one thing I can count on you for, it's that you'll always break my heart if given the chance." I cleared my throat, fighting back tears. "I followed you to the restaurant, and I saw her. I didn't know her name or anything about her until my first day. Even then, we don't see each other's last names at work. The next day, I told Christina I needed a few weeks off, and I applied at the restaurant."

"Do you realize how insane that is?" he asked, shaking his head. "Look, I get that what I did was wrong, but don't the two of you realize this is insane? This confrontation? How far you've all gone to catch me red-handed? I mean, what now? What does any of it matter? I've said I'm sorry, but what good does it do? Do you feel better knowing the truth? Maybe I was protecting you by not telling you."

I shook my head. "You were protecting yourself, and you know it."

"It's why you never told us the truth about your

parents," Amma said. "How long were you going to keep making up excuses about why your daughter couldn't see her grandparents after you moved us down here to be near them? You were really never planning to tell us, were you? You pocketed the insurance money and kept it for yourself. Meanwhile, both your *wives* struggled paycheck to paycheck. You know what I've had to do to keep the mortgage and bills paid, even with Phil's help, which I hate accepting. All the side jobs... How could you live with yourself, knowing I was out there doing all I could? Meanwhile, you had enough to pay Phil back and get the house in our name? I don't even have a car, Joe. I was taking the bus until Phil moved in and let me start driving his."

"So what? You had to take a few pictures of yourself. That was your choice! It's not my fault we struggled. I always paid my half of the bills, in two different households. Neither of you was owed that insurance money. It was mine! From my parents." He shoved his finger into his chest adamantly.

"Is that why you killed them?" Amma asked, breaking our rules and bringing that up before I was ready.

"What?" Joe's jaw went slack.

"For the money? Did they *owe* you, Joe?"

He spoke with a breathy tone. "You're insane. You have no idea what you're talking about..."

"Two falls down the stairs on the same afternoon is quite the coincidence," she said with a shrug. "But I guess the police believed it could've been a coincidence. Of course, they weren't taking into account that your first wife had died the exact same way. Poor Lizzie."

She cocked her head to the side, and I watched his expression shift from horror to indignation. His lips formed a thin line. "Did she *owe* you, too? Hm? You always told me that was an accident, that she'd slipped over some laundry at the top of the stairs, but once Edith told me about your parents, I began to put it all together."

She clicked her tongue. "Classic mistake, Joe. Killers have to change up their MO. You'd know that if you watched TV with me every once in a while. Then again, I guess you had your hands pretty full with your two families."

"Half your week with me, half your week with your wife and child... It was perfect, really," I said. "Until we started asking questions. Coming at you from both directions with the accusations and the suspicions."

"Were you planning to kill one of us next? When the money ran out?" Amma asked the question I'd been too afraid to ask myself.

Something flickered in his eyes that terrified me, something that resembled a confirmation. "So, what are you going to do? Turn me in? You have no proof," he spat. "I've never laid a finger on either of you, and all three deaths were ruled accidental. Because that's what they were."

"Oh, no, Joe. We'd never turn you in," Amma said in a singsong voice. "We know how good of a liar you are. It's like we've said, we need to catch you red-handed."

He glanced at me, then took a step back. "What do you mean?"

"It all started with the app," she told him. "The texting app has actually come in quite handy."

It took him a moment. Then realization washed over his face. "Wait a minute..." He pointed to her, then me, then back to her. "*You* sent those messages to yourself?"

"*We* did," she said, wagging a finger between the two of us.

"Why?" He took another step backward, his legs bumping into the sofa.

She wrinkled her nose playfully. "Let's call it... painting a narrative. Add that to the fact that I called them over to the house last night and claimed that you were banging on the door, scaring Zoe. I showed them the texts you sent, telling me you were coming over after I asked you not to. And, since it's Phil's house and not ours, I had every right to ask you to stay away."

"I never came by the house."

"You did." She batted her eyes innocently. "I have the police report to prove it. I'm in the process of filing for a restraining order, too, just in case."

"And I brought Dan over last night when I knew she'd be calling the police, so we have extra witnesses. We know there was a disturbance. Amma was so shaken up she couldn't go to work today."

"What does Dan have to do with any of this?" he snarled.

"Like she said, we're painting a narrative. We switched the account where your monthly charge goes through from the account you share with Amma to the account I had access to. When I pulled it up and conveniently noticed the charge in front of him, we had reason to investigate. I had to make it all seem innocent enough. Dan and I practically discovered it together, even if I had to nudge us in the right direction. So now, he's seen the messages, too. He's seen the police showing up. He knows we had a fight today. He knows you've been cheating. He knows what kind of man you are. We all do."

"You're all fucking insane." He waved an arm manically. "You can't just do this. You can't just—"

"Lie?" Amma asked. "Like you do?"

"The police will see what we want them to see now. They'll see who you really are," I told him, nodding slowly.

"What? Because you pretended I said you were crazy? Because you said I tried to get into my house? So, what? Neither of those is a crime."

"Bigamy is," Amma said. "Murder is."

He swallowed. "Those messages don't prove

anything." A sudden confidence filled his expression. "And you know what? File your stupid restraining order. Who cares? If you think I want anything to do with either of you after this, you're more insane than I thought. You've got no proof of anything. I'll tell them the truth, and then it'll be your word against mine. I'll take my chances with that. Like you said, I'm a good liar. And, even if you can get me convicted for bigamy, it's what? A few months in jail? Maybe?"

"You know, he's right," I said, earning a relieved look from Joe. "Jail isn't punishment enough." The relief disappeared.

"We've got to catch him red-handed," Amma repeated.

"What do you mean?" Joe's eyes widened.

"Oh, we didn't show you, did we?" My lips upturned into a smile that didn't quite fit my mood. The hairs on my arms stood on end.

"Show me what?"

"The last message you sent Amma."

"What the hell are you talking about?"

I slid my phone from my pocket, holding out the app so he could read the last message. "You invited her here. You thought I was going to be at Dan's, and you invited Amma to come over so you could talk. Away from her brother. Away from Zoe."

He glanced between us, opening his mouth to speak, but Amma cut him off.

"Only, you weren't planning on just *talking*." She

grinned. "See, you'd realized you had one wife too many. And since I was your only *legal* wife, the only one you'd be able to get an insurance policy on, it made sense that I was the one you tried to take out."

He stepped toward her, his hands balled into fists. "Now, wait a minute. I never—"

"Not another step." With stunning ease, she lifted the gun from her purse and into the air, pointing it directly at his face.

His hands went up, stepping back in defeat. "Whoa. Jesus. What the hell, Amma? What the hell are you doing with that?"

"What am *I* doing? Don't you mean what are *you* doing?" she asked innocently.

"You were going to kill her, Joe," I said softly. "Just like you killed your parents. Just like you killed your first wife."

"You're both nuts. Absolutely batshit." He stepped back, shaking his head. "I've had enough of this." He headed for the door, but she stepped in front of him.

"Don't think you want to do that."

"What are you going to do? Shoot me? Really? Then it'll be *you* going to prison. Zoe will be without a mom. Is that really what you want?"

He'd rattled her, but she composed herself quickly, the worry evaporating from her expression, the wrinkle in her forehead smoothing itself out. "I'm just here because you asked me to be. You're the one who brought your gun. You're the one pointing it to my head right now."

"What are you..." He trailed off, trying to make sense of what we were saying.

"I wasn't supposed to be home," I said again. "But I didn't think you would be, either. We'd had a fight because you didn't think we could afford a baby, and I asked you for some space. I found out you were having an affair, and we had a very public fight in front of my place of work. I was staying with a friend. You weren't supposed to be here."

"What are you talking about?" he asked, pleading with me, tears in his eyes.

"But when I came back to the apartment tonight to get a few things, I heard voices. Screams. Crying. You were shouting at her so loudly. It scared me. I didn't know what to do."

"What is happening right now?" It seemed he'd finally begun to catch on.

"When I came inside, you had her gunned down on the ground. I didn't even know you had a gun. We didn't keep them in our apartment."

"But you kept one at our house," she said. He spun back around to face her, his back to me. "I didn't even notice it was missing. When you asked me to meet you here after I'd confronted you about having an affair, I thought it was strange, but I wanted our marriage to work, so I would've done anything. We have a daughter. Another baby on the way. I loved you so much, Joe.

I just couldn't see the truth about who you were until I had the barrel of a gun pointed at my face."

He waved his hands at his sides. "Stop this. Both of you just stop, okay? You've made your point..."

Amma went on, unfazed. "When I got here, you'd been drinking. You were crying. The gun lay on the table. I tried to run, but you were faster than me. Stronger. You grabbed me, threw me down on the ground. You told me if I moved, you'd shoot me. I loved you. I never thought you'd want to hurt me."

"I do love you," he whimpered.

"You told me you didn't have a choice. You told me you wished there was any other way. I felt like I was going to be sick. I pleaded with you, begged you to think about the baby. To think about Zoe." Her voice cracked as she said the last sentence.

"I didn't..."

"You told me you'd make it painless. That you'd take care of Zoe. I had no choice. If I moved, I knew you'd kill me. I closed my eyes, praying for death. Praying it would be painless. Praying our babies would be okay."

"Why are you doing this?" he bellowed, tears painting his cheeks.

"And then she heard the door," I said, my voice barely above a whisper. "I came home. I saw you. I understood what was happening."

"You pointed the gun at her," Amma said. "My coworker. But suddenly, I was starting to piece it together. You said now you didn't have a choice. You were going to kill us both. Save yourself. You said something about making it look like a break-in. There was talk of insurance money, but we didn't understand. We were so scared, Joe..."

"So scared," I agreed. "We had no choice. You were distracted."

"You'd turned to face her, but I started pleading with you," Amma said. "You pointed the gun at me. You said I'd go first."

"I... I g-grabbed th-the first thing I saw..." I knew what I was supposed to say next, what I was supposed to do next, but I couldn't breathe. Suddenly, my chest was constricting, my vision blurring with tears.

Joe spun in circles, trying to keep up with what we were saying and which of us was talking. Amma waited for me to finish what I was trying to say, but I couldn't. I placed a hand to my chest, lightning-sharp pain shooting through it.

Breathe...

Breathe...

Breathe...

I was suffocating.

"I grabbed the f-f-first thing I s-s-aw..." I repeated, fighting for every breath and every syllable.

"The first thing *you*—" he jolted, the last part of the sentence coming out high pitched and painful as he shot forward, head first, his body contorting in a rigid, unnatural way as it plummeted downward. His eyes widened as his knees slammed to the ground, and he fell forward. Behind him, Amma stood, horror-struck, holding the remnants of the snow globe Joe had given me just days before. She dropped it, and it plunged downward, landing on the floor with a loud *THUMP*.

She glanced at her bloody palm, then at me. "Red-handed," she repeated once more. The word that had become our anthem as we plotted and planned this entire thing.

Glass shards decorated his hair, the glittery water from the globe swirling and mixing with the blood as it pooled from the wound at the base of his skull, staining the collar of his gray sweater. His eyes were open, staring blankly into space, pain-free and oblivious to the mess he'd left behind.

His scent hit me then, maybe for the first time. The scent that had once made me feel so safe. The scent that I'd never experience again.

He was gone.

Joe was gone.

I fell to the ground, my knees cracking against the linoleum, but I couldn't be bothered to care. I couldn't breathe. Couldn't think.

Joe would never breathe or think again.

What had we done?

What had we done?

Amma, sensing my panic, moved toward me, lifting her face upward in an attempt to get me to look at her. "Hey, it's okay."

"I'm sorry. I c-couldn't…"

"Nope. It's okay. I had you. I took care of it."

I trembled, rocking back and forth on my knees as I tried to breathe, watching as the blood spilled farther down onto his sweater, spreading in strange shapes and patterns—ink blots on a canvas. I imagined I'd never be able to look at a Rorschach test the same way.

We'd planned this.

It was how it was supposed to go, but that didn't make it any easier.

Had we actually understood the gravity of what we were doing? I wasn't sure.

I watched the man I loved bleeding out onto the floor, unable to move, unable to breathe or think. It felt as if I'd died right along with him.

This was what I wanted in that it was my only choice, but it wasn't what I wanted. Not really.

Amma leaned her face over, blocking my view of him. "Breathe," she instructed. "You're going to go into shock if you don't breathe."

I thought I had been breathing, but apparently not, because even after she'd said it, she moved closer to me yet again, careful not to touch me with either her bloody hand or the one that still held the gun. "Edith, breathe. It's going to be okay. We had to do this." She nodded, willing me to agree. "We had to do this, or he was going to do it to us. He all but admitted that. He was a horrible person. He didn't care about us." She glanced down at my belly. "We had to do it for our children. They need us."

I nodded, brought back to reality at the mention of my child. "I, um, I should call 911."

"Not yet," she said. "Wait until he's gone."

"He's not..."

"Not yet." She shook her head, glancing back at him. "It won't be long." She had tears in her eyes as she said it, despite her calm and cool demeanor. "We've got each other's backs, right? The plan works as long as we stick to it."

I licked my lips, huffing out a breath. "Yes."

"Okay..." She seemed wary, but she had no reason to. At the end of the day, she was right. She'd been right when we made the decision, and she was right now.

This was the only way.

The police had to catch Joe red-handed. He could never get the chance to lie to them the way he had us. He'd tried to kill her. We'd acted in self-defense. There was no other choice.

Though the details were wrong, it wasn't actually all that far from the truth.

She bent down next to him, placing the bloody hand on his neck to check for a pulse. She closed her eyes for what felt like an eternity before she hung her head, a tear dripping from the end of her nose. "He's gone."

The air was sucked out of the room, and suddenly

we were moving in real time again. I pulled my phone out once again, swiping my nose with the back of my hand and dialing 911 with trembling fingers. She cleaned her prints off the gun with the corner of her shirt before placing it in his hand, pressing down each of his fingers hard enough to leave prints. When she released it, his hand was limp, the gun resting in his palm.

She stood, nodding at me once more.

"It's done," she said, watching as my thumb hovered over the button that would connect us to the help we'd both so desperately needed.

Sometimes we keep secrets from the people we love to protect ourselves.

Sometimes we do it to protect them.

I thought about that as I pressed the button and relayed the story to the dispatcher on the other line, and as Amma and I sat on the edge of my couch, arms linked together, both trembling as we waited for the police to arrive.

I thought about secrets, and about the people my secrets—*our* secrets—would protect. Joe's secrets were selfish, meant only to protect himself. But Amma and me? Our secrets would protect our children, our families. They'd protect any future women Joe might've left as brokenhearted and destroyed as we were. They'd protect Dan, the best friend I didn't deserve and the one I could tell almost anything, but not this. I couldn't let him risk his life to help me carry this out, even though I knew he would've in a heartbeat. And, selfishly, our secrets would protect us, too.

From our own mistakes.

From the man we thought we loved. The man we thought loved us.

We'd carry our secrets forward, never speaking them aloud, not even to each other ever again. As I looked at Amma, offering her a small smile, something told me that despite all Joe had taken from me, he'd given me a few things, too.

A child, first and foremost.

A friend.

A belief in myself I'd almost lost.

"We didn't have a choice," she said after a while, sounding unsure.

I shook my head just as I heard the sounds of heavy footsteps coming toward my door.

"We did," I told her, remembering something Jenna had told me once and finally seeing the truth in that. "There's always a choice. We chose this."

We stood, hands locked together as we moved to open the door for the officers. We clung to each other for dear life, ignoring the trembling bodies and tears that fell. Ignoring the pain we felt and hoping somehow, someday, it would subside.

———

THE NEXT FEW HOURS, days, and months were a blur.

Statements and questionings, moving out of the apartment and in with Dan, doctor's appointments for the baby, and finding a new job. Dan surprised me by replacing the snow globe we'd broken, and Nick helped me paint the bedroom I'd taken over at their apartment. I was starting to find my place again, as tough as it was.

I saw Amma a few times during those months. While we weren't exactly friends now, I knew we were closer than most people who heard our story would expect us to be. In all reality, we should've been enemies.

That was another reason the plan worked so well; who would ever suspect the wife and the mistress of working together?

As the months passed, we checked in with each other from time to time. I introduced her to Dan and Nick, and she introduced me to her daughter and Phil. In a weird way, we'd been forever bonded by what happened. So, I'd take what I could get with her. Whatever our weird new relationship was—the bonding over our pregnancies while containing a horrible secret—it was nice. She filled a void that had been left by Joe, and I think I did the same for her.

Once the investigation had officially closed and his death was ruled as self-defense, the two of us were free to carry out our lives without repercussions—legal ones, anyway. That day felt like a dozen sunsets in paradise. A cotton candy fountain. A full day's binge of

The Office. It was the happiest and most free I'd ever felt.

Safety.

True safety for the first time in so long.

The ruling was the last piece of the puzzle I needed to pop into place before I could truly begin living my new life.

The life I'd chosen.

Because I was right when I told Amma there's always a choice. There is.

For so long, I'd let my choices—choices to walk away from my miserable marriage or to ask more questions, choices to stand up for myself or believe in my own worth, choices to trust my gut or listen to my instincts—pass me by.

But now, my life was mine.

I'd fought for it.

Killed for it, in fact.

And, if I had to do it all over again, I wouldn't even think twice.

For the first time in so long, I could see the forest for the trees, and I'd finally gained the courage to drop the match.

DON'T MISS THE NEXT
PSYCHOLOGICAL THRILLER FROM
KIERSTEN MODGLIN

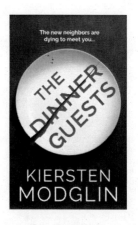

Six friends.
A lifetime of secrets.
One terrifying game.

Order *The Dinner Guests* now:
mybook.to/thedinnerguests

ENJOYED TELL ME THE TRUTH?

If you enjoyed this story, please consider leaving me a quick review. It doesn't have to be long—just a few words will do. Who knows? Your review might be the thing that encourages a future reader to take a chance on my work!

To leave a review, please visit:

mybook.to/tmtt

Let everyone know how much you loved *Tell Me the Truth* on Goodreads:

https://bit.ly/32Twfvn

DON'T MISS THE NEXT RELEASE
FROM KIERSTEN MODGLIN

Thank you so much for reading this story. I'd love to invite you to sign up for my mailing list and text alerts so we can be sure you don't miss my next release.

Sign up for my mailing list here:
kierstenmodglinauthor.com/nlsignup

Sign up for my text alerts here:
kierstenmodglinauthor.com/textalerts

ACKNOWLEDGMENTS

First and foremost, to my incredible husband and wonderful little girl—thank you for all you do for me. Thank you for believing in me, for cheering me on, and for celebrating every success. Thank you for listening to me ramble about plots that may or may not ever be written and not complaining when I lock myself away in the writer's cave for too many hours because I've had a breakthrough. I love you both too much to put into words, which, for a writer, is really saying something.

To my bestie, Emerald O'Brien—thank you for your friendship, your words of advice, the late night talks, the hard questions, the laughs, and for always, always having my back. I love you, friend.

To my immensely talented editor, Sarah West— thank you for working so tirelessly to make my stories the best they can be. I'm so grateful for your insights and advice time and time again.

To the proofreading team at My Brother's Editor— after all this time, I wouldn't trust anyone else to be the final set of eyes on my work. Thank you for believing in my stories and polishing them until they shine.

To my loyal readers (AKA the #KMod Squad)—

thank you, thank you, thank you! I couldn't do this without you guys. I have the best readers in the world. I firmly believe that. Thank you for the reviews, the social media tags and shoutouts, the emails, the recommendations, the excitement for every single new story, and the pure joy you bring to our group every day. You're the reason I get to live my dream and I'm so thankful for each of you.

To my book club—Sara, both Erins, June, Heather, Dee, and Rhonda—thank you for making Wednesday nights fun, for encouraging me to add an extra special character into this story, and for always being ready for the next book. I'm so grateful to know you all.

Last but certainly not least, to you—thank you for purchasing this book and supporting my art. Whether this was your first Kiersten Modglin book or just one of many, I hope it was everything you hoped for and nothing like you expected. Thanks for reading!

ABOUT THE AUTHOR

KIERSTEN MODGLIN is an Amazon Top 30 bestselling author of psychological thrillers, a member of International Thriller Writers, Novelists, Inc., and the Alliance of Independent Authors. Kiersten is a KDP Select All-Star, a recipient of ThrillerFix's Best Psychological Thriller Award and *Suspense Magazine*'s Best Book of 2021 Award. Kiersten grew up in rural western Kentucky with dreams of someday publishing a book or two. With more than thirty books published to date, Kiersten now lives in Nashville, Tennessee with her husband, daughter, and their two Boston Terriers: Cedric and Georgie. She is best known for her unpredictable psychological suspense. Kiersten's work is currently being translated into multiple languages and readers across the world refer to her as 'The Queen of Twists.' A Netflix addict, Shonda Rhimes superfan, psychology fanatic, and *indoor* enthusiast, Kiersten enjoys rainy days spent with her nose in a book.

Sign up for Kiersten's newsletter here:
kierstenmodglinauthor.com/nlsignup

Sign up for text alerts from Kiersten here:
kierstenmodglinauthor.com/textalerts

kierstenmodglinauthor.com
www.facebook.com/kierstenmodglinauthor
www.facebook.com/groups/kmodsquad
www.twitter.com/kmodglinauthor
www.instagram.com/kierstenmodglinauthor
www.tiktok.com/@kierstenmodglinauthor
www.goodreads.com/kierstenmodglinauthor
www.bookbub.com/authors/kiersten-modglin
www.amazon.com/author/kierstenmodglin

Widow Falls

Missing Daughter

The Reunion

The Dinner Guests

ARRANGEMENT NOVELS

The Arrangement (Book 1)

The Amendment (Book 2)

THE MESSES SERIES

The Cleaner (The Messes, #1)

The Healer (The Messes, #2)

The Liar (The Messes, #3)

The Prisoner (The Messes, #4)

NOVELLAS

The Long Route: A Lover's Landing Novella

The Stranger in the Woods: A Crimson Falls Novella

THE LOCKE INDUSTRIES SERIES

The Nanny's Secret

Made in United States
North Haven, CT
09 May 2024

52314388R00162